CW00518053

LETTI PARK

ALSO BY JUDITH HERMANN

LETTI PARK

JUDITH HERMANN

Translated from the German by
Margot Bettauer Dembo

THE CLERKENWELL PRESS

For Christiane

Published in Great Britain in 2018 by
THE CLERKENWELL PRESS
An imprint of Profile Books Ltd
3 Holford Yard
Bevin Way
London WC1X 9HD
www.profilebooks.com

First published in 2016 as *Lettipark* by Fischer Verlag, Germany
Copyright © Judith Hermann, 2016, 2018
Translation copyright © Margot Bettauer Dembo, 2018

The translation of this work was supported by a grant from the Goethe-Institut which
is funded by the German Ministry of Foreign Affairs

10 9 8 7 6 5 4 3 2 1

Printed and bound in Great Britain by Clays, St Ives plc

The moral right of the author has been asserted.

Typeset by MacGuru Ltd in Granjon

A CIP catalogue record for this book is available from the British Library.

ISBN 978 1 78125 840 8
eISBN 978 1 78283 353 6

Contents

Coal

The coal came that morning. We'd got up early and put the last of the wood into the stove; then we went to stand out on the street in front of the house with our hands in our jacket pockets, freezing in the morning fog, watching the clouds formed by our breath. The coal arrived punctually; we signalled to the dump truck to come through the narrow alley between the barn and the tractor shed and as close as possible to the stable in which for years no animal had been housed. The briquettes clattered down onto the winter grass, a big pile, good coal, hardly any broken pieces, and silvery coal dust rose into the air.

We spent the morning shovelling coal from the lawn

into the barn. Seven tonnes of coal; we used shovels and pitchforks, and at first we formed a chain, but then that seemed pointless, and each of us went ahead working on his own. The fog dissipated, and the sun came out; we caught sight of a few wary birds in the bare branches of the bushes. Around noon we took a break. We made coffee and sat down on the stable doorsill that had been worn by the feet of people looking after their animals decades ago. We drank the coffee and talked about how long the new supply of coal would last. Seven tonnes – seven winters? We said, Depends on the winter; and we thought of last winter, which had been incredibly cold and long, an icy winter with snow that lasted into May. We compared the present winter with previous winters, and we talked about possible signs: the tree bark had been especially thick this year, and there had been more nuts than in previous years; we said, Maybe this winter would be even colder than the last. But with this new supply of coal nothing could happen to us. With seven tonnes of coal in the barn we were safe.

After we'd finished our coffee, we dumped the grounds on the grass. For a moment longer we continued to sit on the doorsill; our work was almost done; there wasn't much coal left outside, only a semicircle like a barricade around us.

Vincent came into the yard riding his bicycle through the gate to the street that we hadn't yet closed after the dump truck left. Vincent was four years old; as far as we knew he would soon be five. He came swerving around the corner and saw us immediately, and he rolled towards us on his bike through the alley between the barn and the tractor shed, stopping on the other side of the coal barricade. He was wearing a green jacket, a neatly tied scarf, and a hat, and he didn't have a runny nose. He sat on his bike with his crossed arms propped on the handlebars as if he were fifteen years old, not just four.

He looked at us and said, What are you doing. Matter-of-factly. He said it quite matter-of-factly, and we said, We've been waiting for you; we're shovelling coal; you can give us a hand.

Vincent's mother died last winter. His father had left her, and as a result at first she had a nervous breakdown and then she got sick. Or the other way around: She first got sick and then had a nervous breakdown, but this didn't matter because with her death it all came to the same thing. She had had a protracted case of the flu, and then her heart was affected and because of that she had a stroke, then another, and a third, and eventually they stopped counting the strokes. She had lain in the hospital for three months and towards the end she was blind, could no longer speak, and was able to move only her left foot; the doctors had measured her brainwaves and were of the opinion that in some mysterious way she was still there, and they called this condition being-locked-inside-oneself. Vincent's mother had locked herself up inside herself when Vincent was four years old.

We were sitting with our empty coffee cups in the wintry

midday sun, facing the barricade of coal. We were hot
from working and wide awake. We talked with Vincent;
we asked him if, on his way to our place, he'd been stopped
by the beaver; we told him that the beaver stopped any
children going too fast on their bicycles and told them to
slow down. But Vincent was no fool. He said, That's a lot
of rubbish, and he got so angry that we stopped talking to
him that way. We watched him, as he sat there on his bike,
rolling back and forth a little, and suggested that he could
get his little wheelbarrow and help us get the last of the coal
into the stable; he looked like someone who was missing an
invisible half; but he also looked like someone enveloped
by half a halo.

We thought of his mother who had been an attractive
woman, tall and fragile, with an inimitable, awkward way
of moving her long legs, like a foal. She had always made a
wistful impression, but at times we had heard her ranting,
and then she sounded anything but helpless. In the first
weeks of her illness, we visited her in the hospital ward
where she was lying; by that time she was already blind and
kept saying, It's too bad that I can't see your beautiful faces.

It's too bad that I can't see your beautiful faces.

We hadn't known that for Vincent's mother our faces
had been beautiful, and we went home with the realisation
that there are some things you can only say after they're
gone forever.

Vincent got off his bike and let go of it. He picked up a

piece of coal, turned it this way and that, checking it out, then he climbed over the rampart, walked right through the middle of our group and dropped it on the pile in the corner of the stable. He came back, casually holding on to us for support. After his mother had died, he had asked his father how long death would last; his father had told us that.

Vincent said, I think I'll forget about the wheelbarrow. I can help you without the wheelbarrow too.

And so we got up from the doorsill, took a few steps to exercise our legs and, with our hands on the backs of our hips, we stretched in the winter sun; then we continued. We got the rest of the coal into the stable; we formed another chain, and Vincent helped us. His mother had shown us that one could die of love. She had been living proof that one can die of a broken heart; she had locked herself inside herself out of love. It was odd to think that this would govern Vincent's entire life, and we took the coal from his little dirty hands like holy wafers.

Fetish

There's a fire behind the circus caravan when Ella comes back from the river, but she can't see Carl anywhere. Maybe Carl has left again. The fire has been neatly made, equal-sized pieces of wood carefully laid against each other; it isn't smoky, is burning cleanly and will keep burning for quite a while. Carl has piled up fresh wood against the edge of the fireplace, a circle of fieldstones that have turned white from the ashes. The cut edges of the wood are light-coloured; the wood is not heavy. Next to it there's brushwood. On the folding chair by the fireplace, a blanket.

The circus caravan is old, painted red and blue; the paint is flaking. At the narrow end a stairway leads up to the door;

two little windows face the meadow. Thistles and faded dandelions grow in profusion around the wheels. Ella goes up the steps and opens the door; it's possible Carl has gone to lie down; she knows he hasn't. The bed is made and empty. It's warm inside the caravan. Carl has also lit the stove. The furnishings are simple, a folding table, two chairs, one of which is standing outside next to the fire. The stove in the corner, a clothesline stretching from one wall to the other, and on the shelf above the bed, one single book, a creased, dog-eared copy of *The Death Ship* by Traven. Ella's suitcase stands next to the door. Carl's backpack isn't there, but that doesn't mean anything; he always takes the backpack with him, never lets it out of his sight.

Ella leans against the open door for a while, looking into the caravan. The wind causes a draft in the stove. A spider waits in the web above the folding table. The inside of the caravan smells of the two of them. She closes the door, goes down the stairs and sits on the folding chair by the open fire. Far away, the lights are on in the house on the other side of the unmowed meadow; the other circus caravans, all in a row but a certain distance apart from one another, are dark. When Carl and Ella arrived in the afternoon, they saw a skeletal figure, all skin and bones, wearing a sari and tattooed up to her neck, sitting on the stairs leading up to the caravan next to theirs; she had jumped up and fled into her caravan as if they had interrupted her in the performance of some basic function. Now the door is locked; above it, something decorated with feathers and branches is turning in the wind; from a distance it looks like the skull of an animal – a ferret? A rat, a weasel. The fire hisses. Ella can hear the birds down by the river, the hard beating of their wings. Graylag geese; on her way down to the river she had startled them in the meadows along the banks, and they had risen in swarms and circled over the water, clamouring and honking. The land on the other side of the river was wild and uninhabited. In the distance, a tower. Not a soul in sight. The river was flowing fast, full of eddies and whirlpools in the middle. It was already too cold to go into the water. She had walked for a while downstream, then turned and come back.

And so she simply continues to sit by the fire. She definitely won't go over to the house, or go over there to those other people; she doesn't know them at all; they're people Carl knows. He had introduced Ella to the others, just briefly; he had left it up to her either to sit down with them or to go back to their own caravan. Up close, the skeletal figure, a girl – her tattoos depicting a swarm of blowfish with bristling spines – turned out to be unexpectedly approachable, as did the extraordinarily large man to whom the house, the caravans, the meadow belonged. People who had an intense way of looking at you. People with eyes like hot coals. Barefoot, suntanned children, women wearing amulets around their necks, and a blind old man with a carved sceptre. Water carafes filled with stones stood on the long table – amethyst and rose quartz; the tattooed girl answered Ella's question about the stones, looking past her and pronouncing the words deliberately and meaningfully. In a corner of the room, a rainmaker; above the stove, a shrine to Buddha. Faded Tibetan prayer flags hung suspended between the birch trees in front of the house. There was nothing objectionable. But in spite of that Ella had gone back to her caravan, and she'll now remain sitting there; she has a feeling that Carl would want it that way, and she also feels he is somewhere nearby, watching her. Watching her from the house or from one of the other caravans or from a hiding place among the trees or the sloppily piled-up stacks of wood. If she does everything right, he'll come back.

When the fire is almost out, she puts on more of the freshly cut wood. Just as Carl did – each piece upright and laid against the others at a slant. For the first time in her life she is keeping a fire going. It's working better than she thought it would; the wood is dry and burns readily. And in spite of that it's difficult because she doesn't want to let the fire get too big; she is afraid that if it gets too big, someone might come to join her; the girl or someone else from the other caravans, or in the worst of cases, the man who owns the house, the caravans and the meadow; the thought that he might come over, relaxed and self-assured, wearing felt boots and a sheepskin over his shoulders, fills Ella with unease. It would be quite impossible for her to be there with him in case Carl were to turn up again. She doesn't know when Carl will come back; actually she doesn't know if he will ever come back, but when and if he comes back and finds her sitting by the fire with that man – by the fire that he, Carl, lit for her – it would be a disaster. So she keeps the fire small. Just big enough to warm her, yet small enough so that it won't attract anyone's attention to her. No one's except Carl's. It works to a certain extent.

It's amazing how dark it gets at some point. Night falls and it is totally dark. The moon is oily; the light in the house at the far end of the meadow is a sharply outlined square. Animals are rustling in the grass around the caravan, and the wind blowing through the trees makes their branches creak. Ella thinks she hears a door in the house slam shut, and cars driving away. She unfolds the blanket and wraps it around herself. She doesn't hear the boy coming, but suddenly he is there. He stands by the fire, across from Ella, and at first his face, illuminated from below, has a predatory look. Then she recognises him; she met him that afternoon; he belongs with someone from one of the other circus caravans, a traveller, as much a stranger here as she herself is. He is maybe seven years old; she has trouble judging children's ages, but she thinks that at this hour he ought to be lying in bed, sleeping.

How late is it?

She says this to him instead of hello, and he shrugs.

She says, Would you like to sit down here with me, and he nods, and she goes and gets the second chair from inside the caravan; apparently her fire is the right size for a little boy. She puts the chair next to hers, and he sits down. His legs dangle just off the ground. He immediately gazes gravely into the fire as if it might go out before he has really observed it, or as if he were afraid that if he doesn't really look into the fire, Ella might send him away. It's clear that, in contrast to her, he has sat at many fires. He poses no problem for Ella. A boy – a little boy with shaggy hair, trousers that are too short, a hoodie and dirty trainers without laces – a little boy like that would not be a problem for Ella if Carl should come back.

Then he takes his eyes off the fire and looks up into the sky. He looks at the caravan; he looks at Ella out of the corner of his eyes. They talk a little. The boy asks Ella how many stars there are, his voice sounding rough and scratchy, and the tone of voice indicating that he already knows the correct answer.

Well, how many stars are there then.

Ella says, Oh, no idea. I have no idea. Infinitely many?

The boy says, in affirmation, Right there, above us, there are a thousand. About a thousand. Then there's the Milky Way too.

And Black Holes, Ella says.

Yes, Black Holes, the boy says. Huge, fat Black Holes. Nobody knows what's on the far side. What's supposed to be inside them.

Ella hesitates; then she says, But the Universe is falling asleep. Did you know that? It's falling asleep; the stars will go out. A lot of them have already gone out.

This prospect seems not to surprise the boy. He nods and says nothing for a while; then he takes a stick and pokes around in the fire. Expertly he adds more wood. Ella finds him unusually serious and quiet in an adult way, but his face is round and still very childlike; he is good-looking. Impossible to ask him about his parents. About school, siblings, friends, what he likes or doesn't like to do. She bides her time; suddenly she feels that in principle she ought simply to wait for everything. If Carl were here, she wouldn't be able to wait for anything; she wouldn't be able to pay any attention to the boy at all; she'd be much too busy with Carl.

For a while the boy pensively imitates the sound of a crackling piece of wood. Piff, paff. Piffpaff. He tilts his head, draws up his shoulders and coughs. Then he says, Do you want a picture.

What kind of picture?

Well, a sort of picture; I cut it out of a newspaper once, and I want to give it away, but nobody wants it.

Ella says, What is there to see in the picture.

The boy says, I don't know.

He says, Should I just show it to you, and when Ella nods, he gets up and dashes off. She's almost certain that he won't come back. That he'll run into another grown-up and be sent to bed, that some new idea will suddenly pop into his head, and he'll forget Ella, her fire, the picture. But he comes back, and she doesn't ask him where he went, where the picture was – in a book, under a mattress, in the kitchen of the house in the middle of the table at which they all sit, nor does she ask him whether he ran into Carl.

The boy comes back quite out of breath as if he'd been running. As if he, for his part, had thought Ella, along with the fire, the circus caravan, and the two folding chairs, might have vanished into thin air. He sits down again on the chair next to her and waits till his breathing has calmed down. Then he pulls a piece of paper out of his trouser pocket. It's been folded more than once and he unfolds it and hands it to Ella without a word.

She leans forward and looks at it. A photomontage – Freud's couch replicated multiple times and placed one behind the other, an image from a dream. No caption. The paper feels sticky.

Ella says, How long have you been carrying this around with you; and the boy says evasively, Oh, I don't know any more. I think a couple of weeks. Quite a while. Anyway, you don't want it either.

No, Ella says firmly. Sorry. I don't want it.

She's sorry, but she really doesn't want it. She thinks he ought to burn it. And finally the boy says of his own accord, I should burn it. Don't you think.

Ella says, That's a good idea. You ought to do that.

She gives the photo back to him, and he crumples it up into a ball and puts the ball into the glowing embers, pushes it into the middle of the fire with his stick. Detached. The ball flares up and melts away. The boy sighs. Ella looks at him sideways. Was this his first sacrifice? His first time. He turns his round head slowly to face her, and his eyes seek hers with a surprising and solemn authority.

Your turn, he says.

The following morning is cool. Windy and sunny. Carl hasn't come back, and Ella is awakened by the cold. She had gone to sleep without adding any coal to the stove, and it went out. She pushes the door open and lets light into the trailer. She puts a sweater on over her nightgown and sits down on one of the steps; it occurs to her that she's sitting there just as the skeletal figure had been the previous day; she thinks, It can happen quickly. The girl's caravan is as quiet as if it were empty and the girl gone. The fire in the fireplace is out; Ella and the boy have burned up all the wood. She'll have to fetch some more wood in case Carl doesn't come back today either and in case she decides to stay in spite of that; she will have to ask the man who owns this universe for it. Awkward, but not impossible. What does Carl expect? The answer to this is important, but she feels that the answer can wait.

The sun rises quickly over the river. The boy comes as silently as the evening before. He is wearing a velvet cape. His movements are sleepy, have a dragged out, exhausted beauty. He doesn't smile, but he stands next to Ella on the steps and she raises her hand and touches his cheek and his hair.

He says, We're leaving.

Ella gazes after him until he disappears among the birches by the house. The Tibetan prayer flags flutter in the wind. There is no one else in sight.

Solaris

Ada and Sophia lived together while they were studying. Sophia was studying drama in college; Ada was training as a photographer. They shared a two-room apartment whose rooms were connected by a French door. Sophia had the room on the left with three windows on two sides of the room; Ada had the one on the right. The right-hand room had two windows, and when they moved in Ada painted her walls blue. Sophia painted her walls white, first folding herself a hat out of newspapers for the paint job. During that time, while they were redecorating the apartment in undershirts and bare feet, Sophia smoking, the paper hat on her head, popular songs playing on the radio – *Dance a Samba with me because dancing a Samba makes us happy* – all five windows wide open, Sophia said, quite offhand, We're going to stay here till we're old and grey and dusty. Till we're ashes and everything is over. Ada! I promise.

Someone had once assured Ada and Sophia that their voices sounded identical; so when the phone rang, and Ada answered and there was somebody on the line she didn't want to talk to, she'd say, Oh, I'm sorry, but Ada isn't here just now. I'll tell her that you called; she'll call you back. OK?

But she never called back.

When fellow students came to visit Sophia, she would spread a white sheet out on the floor of her room and put wine and water and glasses in the middle of it. The drama students came in the evening; they sat down by the white sheet as if they were sitting in the grass under birch trees; grass and birch trees growing around the white sheet. They leaned up against one another; they drank a fair bit, but never too much. Ada stayed in her room. Sophia never closed the French doors. Ada sat at her desk; she could see the others, and late at night after she had turned off the light and was lying on her back awake in her bed, she heard them singing.

Many years later Sophia has an engagement at a big theatre, and Ada comes to the opening night, to the opening night of *Solaris*. She lives in another city, is married and has two children; she sees Sophia only rarely, but they often talk on the phone; they visit each other; they write emails. They make the effort.

Sophia had also married, but then she got divorced. She has three daughters and a Nigerian au pair girl, and now she's living in an apartment that is so large you can get lost in it.

Ada arrives on the overnight train. She had asked Sophia, When do you get up? I don't want to wake you; the train arrives at six in the morning at the main station; I'd be at your place at half past six. Isn't that too early for you?

But Sophia said that she gets up every day at seven o'clock anyway. The children are already up at four. Ada should come directly from the main railway station to her place. Without any delay, without stopping for coffee at some terrible joint, without any detours. Without a detour, Ada. Listen, Sophia had said. Take a taxi.

And so, at seven o'clock Ada is standing in front of Sophia's door. She rings briefly and hesitantly, and of course Sophia doesn't open the door. Ada knew this would happen. It's still half dark; the hallway is a gallery open to the courtyard out back; the leaves of the trees in the court-yard are rustling dramatically in the wind.

There is a chair in front of the door.

It's standing as if placed there for Ada, like a chair on a stage, and so she sits down and waits. Listening, hearing the rustling of the leaves and waiting for Sophia to wake up.

The birthday of Sophia's youngest daughter falls on one of the days Ada is visiting Sophia; she is turning five. Sophia is busy with the final rehearsals; the au pair girl is preparing for the birthday party; the older daughters are at school. Ada is alone much of the time. It rains from morning to night, and she hardly leaves the house. She stays in Sophia's large apartment where she can do whatever she wants; the au pair girl's room, a small bedchamber, is the only one closed to her. The rooms lead into each other; they form a circle. Ada goes from the kitchen through the hall through the daughters' rooms, the living room, the dressing room, Sophia's bedroom, a room that has only an armchair standing in it, a room for a vase of gladioli, and one with a fabulous bookshelf, and then she is back in the kitchen, where the au pair girl who, in Ada's presence, acts as if she were deaf and dumb, is stringing paper garlands from one wall to the other, and filling punch bowls with red berries and tangerine slices. The windows are open as they had been back then; rain drizzles into the rooms.

Everywhere Ada finds traces of their former life together. A photo – the wintry view from Sophia's room out into the grey street. A blouse embroidered with little horses hanging on the clothes rod. A mother-of-pearl barrette. A hashish pipe. A knife. She lies down on the sofa in the otherwise totally empty living room; she lies on her side, her cheek resting on her folded hands; she is so calm that she feels as if she were dissolving, almost forgetting who she is.

The opening night of *Solaris* is on the evening of the youngest daughter's birthday.

Sophia is playing Harey.

Alexander is playing Chris Kelvin. Alexander was at

drama school with Sophia; he was one of the students who used to sit around the white sheet; maybe he was the one who was too much for Ada back then – with his physique as massive as a gladiator's and the sculpted planes of his face.

At breakfast Sophia tells Ada that Alexander cheats on his wife and is forever watching porn on the internet, that in the daytime before rehearsals he meets women from the internet in scruffy hotel rooms down by the train station.

She says, When he stands in front of me at the rehearsals he smells of semen. Of sweat and sex and semen, of the secretions of the aroused genitals of different women. Of cunts.

She says this while she is preparing the lunch boxes for her three daughters; she wraps sandwiches, cookies; she washes small green apples and peels cucumbers and carrots, cuts them into little pieces; she says it nonchalantly, matter-of-factly, almost pleasantly.

Of cunts. She repeats the word, turning it this way and that.

But in the afternoon when Alexander, who has come to drop off one of his children at the birthday party, stands in front of the door, holding his child's hand and a large gift tied with a pink ribbon under his other arm, Ada thinks he manages to conceal all this fairly well. Actually, he smells of soap. His face is open and clean, just as in the past; his expression almost bewildered.

He introduces himself to Ada; he says his name and shakes hands, and Ada says, We already know each other.

She can see that he is trying to remember. That he is doing his best.

Sophia is the most beautiful mother a birthday child could wish for. Absolutely the most beautiful. She is wearing a slim dress and the most wonderfully crafted silvery stockings, sparkling rhinestone earrings, and her hair is severely yet softly combed back from her face. She sways a little in high-heeled shoes, looking festive and serious; she is brave.

Thirteen children arrive. The au pair hangs up their jackets and puts the bouquets of flowers into vases; she blindfolds the children and places marshmallows under old pots. Torn wrapping paper rustles on the floor, puffed rice crackles. The older daughters have withdrawn to their rooms and are on their phones. The youngest daughter has red cheeks and is trembling with excitement. There are chocolate muffins, jelly-filled doughnuts, a strawberry tart, whipped cream, punch and cream puffs. Alexander stays. Sophia opens a bottle of champagne, and they clink glasses. The au pair finally stops watching them and arranges the room for a game of musical chairs. One of the children is picked up early and cries bitterly. The champagne is ice cold, and for Ada it turns the afternoon into something that hurts behind the ears, hurts in certain places in her body where, she suspects, happiness is hiding.

Alexander and Ada have a conversation that she will recall later as having gone something like this:

Alexander says, And what do you do. What are you up to these days.

I take photographs, Ada says. She says it with exactly

the same intonation, the same insecure manner and idiotic indecision as fifteen years earlier.

I still take photographs; I try to make a living with it; it's going pretty well.

What do you photograph, Alexander says. His expression indecipherable.

Ada says, People? And places. Water. A bowl. A child. I can't describe it for you. But you can look it up on the internet. I've heard you know your way around there.

Ada has no idea why she said that. She can't believe she really said it. Alexander's gaze rapidly, very pointedly, turns to Sophia at the other end of the living room where the party favours are being snatched out of her hands, and then back again to Ada.

He says, speaking slowly, Yes, I know my way around. You mean I can look at your photos on the internet. Download one for my stash.

She remembers how they both burst out laughing. Gasping for breath with hands raised. And on Ada's part, with a pounding, racing heart.

Ada is allowed to stay with Sophia. And to leave the birthday party together with Sophia and Alexander; driving through the rain in a taxi to the theatre, to stay in Sophia's dressing room and to watch as Sophia turns into Harey. As she changes from the mother of a birthday child into Harey, as she whispers, Does that mean that I am immortal? Does that mean that I ... am immortal. The assistant producer knocks and brings in a sumptuous bouquet of white roses;

she brings good wishes for the premiere and good luck charms, spits three times over Sophia's shoulder, careful not to spit over her shoulder while on the threshold. On the loudspeaker above the make-up mirror, the stage manager summons the actors to the stage. Ada stands near the technicians; the animated, tense murmuring of the audience comes through the closed curtain. It's hot on the stage. The objects on the stage are either in disorder or already weightless, a field cot, a space module, a control console, a microphone, a folding screen, all enveloped in an artificial fog.

Alexander has turned into Chris Kelvin.

He is wearing a golden space suit; he stretches his hand out to Ada. He walks over to her, takes his helmet off again, and kisses Ada on the mouth; he gives her a cosmonaut's kiss.

There are no bridges between Solaris and Earth, whispers Sophia standing next to Ada.

There cannot be any.

She says, Ada, we're starting now. You have to leave. We are starting.

Poems

I used to visit my father once or twice a year. On my last visit I brought him some cake; it was mid-summer, and I bought a piece of plum tart and a piece of apricot tart at the pastry shop café next to the house where he had been living for some time. The tarts and cakes in the glass cases looked gorgeous, and all the tables in the café section were occupied. People were eating large pieces of cake, drinking iced coffee, iced chocolate or tea from dainty white porcelain cups. I took a long time choosing. I let a few people go ahead of me. Had there been an empty table, I would gladly have sat down and also ordered an iced coffee. I wanted to delay the visit to my father. I wanted to put it off.

My father lived in a tiny, cluttered apartment that was crammed full of things. An apartment with so much furniture, so many pictures, objects, boxes and crates that there was really no room for my father, which says it all. That was how he wanted it. Exactly this way and no other. He wanted to sit on a packed suitcase in the middle of a stage-set consisting of a chaotic jumble, on top of a heap of rubble; then he could more or less face life's demands. Whenever I went to visit him it was difficult to rustle up even the most basic dishes. Where was the kettle? The last time there was still a dented tin of instant coffee; the tin turned up in a box full of old plaster death masks. The curtains were always closed. Packages and boxes that presumably didn't belong to my father were piled up in the hall. He was wearing two unmatched slippers. He was unshaven; his hair stood on end. On the day I visited him with the plum and the apricot tarts, it was a miracle that we were eventually able to sit down at a table in front of two plates and two cups, and that there was hot, bitter coffee in the cups. There was no milk or sugar.

This spoon, my father said, and pointed with emphasis at the tarnished and bent spoon next to my plate, was your great-grand aunt's. It's a spoon that belonged to your maternal great-grand aunt.

My father had been ill for a very long time. I should add that he had been in a psychiatric institution for many years; again and again he had to have himself readmitted. He wasn't doing well; he couldn't think clearly; he couldn't take care of anything; and everything was too much for him. My father had been ill in this way as far back as I can remember; I can barely remember ever having had a healthy father, and this is probably the reason I left home as soon as I could. I went far away, and the connection was almost broken; my father was in no position to take any interest in my life, and I felt there was no reason to force him to. I visited him now and then in the psychiatric clinic; there he was totally self-absorbed, and later he probably didn't even remember those visits. Back then he practised being able to endure poems. He would try to read a poem without breaking down, and I must say, it proved extraordinarily and surprisingly difficult for him. We practised it together; there wasn't much else that we could have done together in that institution – he had borrowed a fat volume of poetry from the library and would open it at random to a page and ask me to read to him. And there were days when one single line was too much for him, when he couldn't even bear the line 'The seagulls all look as if Emma were their name'; a line like 'We sat under the hawthorn till the night swept us away' would have killed him.

In the end he gave up.

Later he disappeared. He climbed out of the window in the ward's occupational therapy workshop and was gone for quite a while, then when he turned up again, it emerged that he had got surprisingly far. He had been far away, in a city way up north, yet there too he landed in a psychiatric institution, but they didn't want to keep him; there was no room for him. I drove north with my husband and we picked him up. Without ever having discussed such matters with my father, I had married very young, and this was the first time my husband and my father had met. In the middle of the night in a windy car park in front of that institution at the edge of the city, my father climbed into the back of the car, leaving the car door open, and didn't even look at my husband. My father behaved as if my husband were a chauffeur. A taxi driver. He sat in the back seat with an expression on his face like that of an offended child; he was silent during the entire trip, staring out into the night; he said not a single word, except once – once he leaned forward and said:

I'm hungry. I'd like a hot dog.

Only crazy people can pull off stunts like that.

Luckily my husband had no problem with it. He understood, and it's quite possible that he felt sorry for my father.

That day in midsummer when I visited my father for the last time, he eyed the slice of plum tart on his plate with his head tilted to one side for a long time – he had gone for the plum tart; rejected the apricot – and then he put his spoon, about whose origin he had left me in the dark, back on the table.

He said, This piece of tart is from the gay pastry shop.

And I said, Which gay pastry shop.

The gay pastry shop downstairs here, in the building. Next door, my father said. They're gays, homosexuals; you must have noticed; only gay people can bake fruit tarts this way. Whip the cream, decorate and glaze the fruit; only a gay person is able to create this kind of plum tart, or an obscene apricot tart like the one on your plate, a picture-book apricot tart, thought up, mixed and baked by a fag. I walk past that pastry shop sometimes and I'm amazed. Amazed.

I memorised this conversation.

It wasn't a real conversation; it was more like a situation. I could have told my father that I was going to remember it all – make a mental note of it, so as to be able to drag it out again years later, think about it again and maybe under-stand it differently.

While my husband and I were driving to that city in the far north to pick up my father from the psychiatric insti-tution there, we were listening to tacky music on the car radio; the sun went down, and the blinking red lights on the windmill turbine blades lit up; we had brought some coffee with us and wine gums and chocolate, and I was grateful without being able to explain it. Around midnight we were standing, all three of us, at a rest stop around a circular plastic table, my husband, my father and I; we were eating hot dogs with mustard and dry, toasted buns off paper plates, and we didn't let my father out of our sight for even a second because we were afraid he would make use of the first unguarded moment to slip away across the fields. We took him back to the institution from which he had escaped, and I can see myself standing outside the glass door of the ward until the male nurse – he was holding my father gently by the elbow – had walked around the corner at the end of the corridor with my father, and of course my father did not turn around to look at me, and of course I wasn't expecting him to.

But I do remember the ward number – 87. And my father's smell during those years.

My father didn't actually say, I would never buy a piece of cake from that pastry shop. He never said that, but it was probably what he meant.

He ate the entire piece of tart in spite of that; he ate it with that unique, fierce greed that I'd only seen up to that time in old people. He didn't care at all about the gays. I suspect that what mattered was that I had bought a piece of tart for him and that despite everything I somehow knew that he used to love plum tart before he fell ill. It was all about this, and beneath it I'm sure it was also about something else entirely.

Letti Park

How beautiful Elena used to be! A beautiful, slender girl, black eyes, dark brown hair, taut as a bowstring, face flushed as if she were constantly pinching her cheeks. Elena was strong, plucky, cheerful and edgy; she was always on guard. She wore skirts over slacks like a gypsy, cheap jewellery, no make-up, and her hair was as matted as if she had lain in bed all day, smoking, flicking ash on the floor, spreading her legs. Evenings, though, she went to work in a bar on a street with broken cobblestones, dilapidated houses, open front doors, locust trees right and left, and birches in the courtyards. In the winter it smelled of coal and in the summer of gorse and dust. Elena was one of those women who, in the evening, put her hair up into a bun with a pencil. She would put a rust-red skirt on over a pair of mint-green slacks, unlock the bar, and sweep the cigarette stubs out with a broom. She'd fetch herself a beer and switch on the music and the string of coloured lights draped in the branches of the locust tree. Later everyone would come by. Elena was the most beautiful girl on the block.

Elena is standing in front of Rose at the cash register in the market hall; Rose recognises her too late, only after she's already put her strawberries, sugar and cream on the conveyor belt. Had she recognised Elena sooner, she would have gone back and looked for something else to buy, but it's too late for that now. Paul has just come up too and put his things down next to hers, a can of fish, tobacco and a bottle of port. Elena doesn't turn around to look. She's become heavy and old, phlegmatic, slow; yet still unmistakably Elena – almond eyes and hair like snakes, you can tell her skin is warm just by looking, and she has always been taller than all the others – but it seems she's got involved in something. There's someone with her, an Indian – stocky, energetic and strong, maybe with a tendency towards violence and looking a bit down at heel; he has dusty flip-flops on his feet, and his flowered shirt is stained. The Indian straightens out the items on the conveyor belt. Hands them to the cashier and then takes them back from her; he also packs them into a bag; Elena just stands there. Her mind elsewhere. Arms hanging down. Tomatoes, basil in a pot, candles and rice. Cigarettes. Two bottles of whiskey. Elena takes a purse from her bag and opens it like a book. She raises her head and looks at Rose. What does her expression say? Rose can't tell. Elena looks like a sad giantess. A sad, bewitched giantess.

Christ Almighty, Paul says. Dammit. I can't understand the slowness of these people. And the shitty cold in this store. It's like a freezer in here. This is the last time we're ever coming to this place, Rose. You hear me? Strawberries … Your delusional notions about still needing this or that.

Nobody can pronounce the word strawberries with as much contempt as Paul. He leaves Rose standing there and goes over to the newspaper rack; it's not too cold to leaf through the papers. The Indian has become aware of a slight, filament-thin vibration. He takes the purse out of Elena's hand, casting a glowering look at Rose. Does he know how beautiful Elena once was? Does he have the slightest idea? And would things be any different if he did know?

Rose!

Paul is calling to her, and suddenly Elena has become aware of something; she turns her heavy head from Rose to Paul and grasps the connection. Paul is holding up a newspaper, a tabloid in which he's looked up his and Rose's horoscope. For Paul, what Rose's horoscope says is more real and true than anything Rose herself says, and if the horoscope says she should think carefully and finally tell her partner the truth, then Rose can prepare herself for a punishing week. Paul holds up the paper; the headlines report cannibalistic murders, approaching barbarians and rising water prices; he calls over to her, You should take some time off, Rose, slow down a little, and Elena turns her head back towards Rose.

Rose and Elena had nothing in common except that each had caught the eye of Page Shakusky. That each had been an image in Page Shakusky's eyes. A vision. Rose, you see, was attending the university and Page Shakusky discovered her; he had stopped her as she was hurrying home from the university campus with no other goal than to make herself something to eat, to eat at her desk, and to go on studying. Rose had been hurrying past Elena's bar, and Page Shakusky had jumped up from the lopsided garden table where he always sat and had intercepted her. Drunk, of course drunk, in those days he was never sober. He said, What a pretty, graceful girl you are with the walk of a giraffe and the charm of a songbird; everyone is staring at you. Rose didn't fall for any of it. She shook him off and hurried on, ran up the stairs to her apartment, and once there, locked the door from the inside. She allowed Page Shakusky to pay her compliments but she didn't fall for them. Page Shakusky persisted for quite a while. Mornings he would be lying outside her door; after she left her apartment, he would climb up on her balcony and wait for her to come home; he wrote her countless letters full of promises, vows and suggestive remarks. Rose would put her hands over her ears and close her eyes. She was reticent and busy trying to stay afloat in her life, and she knew that Page Shakusky was in reality much the same, except that he had thought up a different strategy. Getting involved with him was quite out of the question. He kept trying for a while longer, and then he stopped because he had discovered another convent-school girl, and then, suddenly, he got involved with Elena. And that was something different. He fell for Elena. Elena seemed to be free of any inclination to surrender. In fact, she seemed to be quite free generally. After six weeks she broke Page Shakusky's heart; she broke it in half and quite casually into two pieces, and then she stuck the pencil back into her hair and switched on the string of coloured lights and sat down outside the door of her bar as if nothing had happened.

The Indian paid for his and Elena's joint purchases. In a way that made it seem as if they had been going shopping together their entire lives, as if he had always paid for himself and Elena. Paul tosses the newspaper back on the pile and comes over to the cash register. The cashier is blonde and young; she picks up the strawberries and looks vacantly into Rose's eyes. Paul is going to ask her what she does; he asks every young cashier the same question.

Rose is reminded of Letti Park. Page's present for Elena, but she can't remember whether Elena had already left him by then or whether she only left him after this present. Left him with or because of this present. Elena had spent her childhood in Letti Park; she had told Page about it. And Page had gone off and photographed Letti Park for Elena. In the winter. An ordinary, dreary park on the outskirts of town, a piece of fallow land, with nothing to see, snowy paths, a deserted circular flowerbed, benches and a vacant lawn. Bare trees, grey sky; that's all there was. But Page had reverently retraced the trail of Elena's childhood. He had gone to see Rose to show her the photos – she was able to open her apartment door to him now that he had stopped his intense, careless courtship of her and was going with Elena – and she left the cup from which he had drunk tea with rum while showing her the photos standing on the kitchen table for days. He had pasted them into a book with great care and written the words, Letti Park, in a wild script on the cover of the book and below that – for Elena. For my Elena. Rose thought that one got a gift like this only once. But in spite of that, Elena walked out on Page sitting with his head down on the lopsided garden table; he was still sitting there in front of the bar, at seven o'clock in the morning, barefoot, eyes red from crying, and drunk. Later he vanished from both their lives. Rose moved away. Elena gave up her bar. The string of coloured light bulbs hung a while longer in the locust tree branches. Rose hasn't been back there for a long time.

What is it you do actually, Paul says to the cashier.

And the cashier blushes delicately and says, I am studying economics; why do you ask?

Rose puts the strawberries, sugar, cream, port, tobacco and the tinned fish into paper bags. Paul points at Rose and says, Her horoscope says she should take some time off, and the cashier laughs and says, We could all use some time off.

In Page Shakusky's book for Elena the park was black

and white with not a soul in sight. A twilight realm. A floating, suspended, celestial world. Vague shadows among the trees and signs on the paths which you couldn't read. Page's nostalgic longing for Elena's childhood, one longing among many.

Rose leaves the bags sitting on the counter and walks out of the supermarket to the car park. The Indian has by now stowed his purchases in the boot of his car; he slams the boot shut, inspects his rear lights, kicks a tyre, then gets in. Elena is already sitting in the car; she's strapped herself in; she's looking straight ahead.

On a piece of paper that Page Shakusky had slipped under Rose's door at four o'clock early one morning back then, there was a sentence she still remembers even today: All the people in my dreams have your face. Page Shakusky had written this sentence to Rose. Even with all his failures, there was something indestructible, something bright about him, and Rose suddenly, ardently hopes that wherever he has ended up he is doing well. It can be enough to have been a face in the dream of another person; it really can be like a blessing, and she hopes that Elena still knows some of that; that Letti Park still matters – the wintry pictures, the promising shadows, the paths into uncertainty.

Behind her the sliding doors open and close again, and Paul comes out and says, What are you waiting for, Rose.

The Indian steps on the gas so abruptly it verges on contempt. Rose takes one step forward; holds up her hand. What is she waiting for?

Witnesses

For Matthew Sweeney

Ivo and I met with Henry and Samantha at a time when our marriage was almost on the rocks. Samantha was going to take over Ivo's job at the Institute; that was the reason for our meeting; they would still be working together there for a while longer, but then Ivo would leave and Samantha would stay on. Henry and Samantha knew that we intended to leave the city for professional reasons; Ivo hadn't mentioned this at the Institute. That was all they knew. Henry and Samantha had just moved here, a couple in a second marriage, grown-up children, the last third of their lives; Henry was considerably older than Samantha. He wore baggy trousers and unironed shirts; his eyes were bloodshot, and he seemed worn out, but when he laughed, his entire face was transformed into that of a pixie, a child-like face; no one seemed to be able to hurt him.

We went to Anice; that year you went to Anice if you wanted to get good fish and couldn't abide waiters who stood at your table and watched arrogantly as you ate. At Anice people drank beer in the front room, and in the back you could go on sitting at the long tables after having eaten, have another bottle of wine in comfortably muted lighting, and talk to one another without having to shout. For Ivo it was awfully depressing; he was terribly sad about all these circumstances, these procedures that seemed to testify to our middle age, our weaknesses. But nothing else had occurred to him. That was the problem; he didn't know what else to do.

At Anice Ivo selected the trout. Samantha and I decided on the halibut. But I'm not so sure about the halibut, Samantha said, and then Henry said that he had once stood in a fish store and heard a lady ask the fishmonger for halibut – he pronounced the word 'lady' deliberately and as if it were his invention, a word without any history. He said, Just like our Samantha here at this table, she had said, What exactly is halibut. And what did the fishmonger say? What did the fishmonger say. The fishmonger said, Dear lady, halibut is the Lamborghini of the seas.

Henry slapped the palm of his hand on the table causing the glasses to jingle and Ivo to flinch. I looked at Samantha. Samantha was looking sideways at Henry. Her shoulder-length hair hung in tightly twirled curls, and she pulled the curls carefully behind one ear, holding on to them so she could see Henry properly, and her look was one of delight.

For my part, Henry said, I'll take the cod. A fabulous local fish caught right outside the door; and apparently he didn't feel he had to look at Samantha, to make sure of her.

Ivo and I were both in our first marriage, and we had one daughter, Ida; I would not be having any more children. Ivo, yes. Ivo would perhaps like to; sometimes I imagined him in a new version – everything starting from scratch; another wife, another house, a new child, a garden with cherry trees and lilacs, and matching porcelain dishes in the kitchen cabinets. And I was certain I wouldn't recognise him any more. I wouldn't recognise Ivo in his new life; he would be someone else; I know this is possible; that we are like that. He would retain his passion for fishing. He would go to illegal dog races on Sundays. He wouldn't stop believing that licking the aluminium covers of yogurt containers caused cancer, and he'd still fall asleep lying on his right side, legs drawn up, one hand between his knees, and he'd say things in his dreams like, Have you checked under this chair, or Please put on something warm and hurry up. But as for all the rest? He would be speaking a different language, like his second child, to whom he would be an old and decidedly indulgent father, and who would have a name that Ivo and I would never ever have chosen. He would eat nuts for breakfast. His birch pollen allergy would

be gone; sex would again be an abyss for him. All this; all
these things. Surprises. But we hadn't got to this point yet.
Back then we were at the point where Ida, coming home
from school, would walk right past us and go to her room,
closing the door behind her and choosing not to eat anything for supper. We were just at the point where Ivo cried
at night. We had it all still ahead of us – the packing of
boxes, the drunken confessions; we were at the beginning
of all that.

The waiter brought the fish and poured more wine. Ivo
looked exhausted, and beads of sweat had formed on
his forehead. He is a good, a prudent and a shy man. He
carried on exactly the sort of conversation that puts you to
sleep – about the inevitable structures at the Institute, then
the stormy spring, then the crisis – but for me it was all
right this way; it was an expression of our circumstances,
our situation.

Henry stayed out of it.

I did too.

Samantha joined in, but after a while she cautiously
changed direction; she started talking a bit about herself.
She said she had been born near the coast and had then
lived for a while far away in the East; she had met Henry
seven years ago, after his marriage ended; she emphasised
that he was not married any more by the time she met him.
Why was she emphasising this point? She said she was
happy to be back.

Henry said he was here because of Samantha. Samantha

was the sole reason for his being here. The only reason for his being on this ghastly, wretched earth at all. He said it matter-of-factly; he was busy with his fish, fiercely filleting it, pushing the skin to the side, and leaving it on the edge of the plate; he sucked each bone clean and appeared utterly content.

He said, Jesus, this fish is talking to me, and he brandished the wine bottle, preparing to refill Samantha's empty glass, but she declined quite pointedly. Ivo, though, raised his glass and held it out to Henry with an expression of submission, and Henry filled it to the brim and they clinked glasses.

They drank a toast to nothing; they left it open.

I no longer remember why Henry started talking about the moon at Anice. Was it because we had just had a full moon? The full moon had brought with it a late spring; it had risen impressively above the roofs of the city and was still there in the clear morning sky at seven. Ivo had called my attention to it that morning before he got into the car to drive to work; we had both stood in front of the house with arms crossed looking up at the moon, so pale and white as if made of Chinese rice paper, and as if it had once belonged to both of us, and that this, for reasons not clear to us, was now over and done with once and for all.

At Anice, Henry said out of the blue that he had once met Neil Armstrong, ages ago, long ago, and I could practically hear Ivo, next to me, immediately beginning to mentally calculate, hear his tortured brain starting to count the years.

I was young back then, Henry said.

And I would have liked to say to Ivo, Just listen for once, it could be enough for you; he was young back then, you don't need to know more than that.

Henry said, I was really young. Good-God-in-heaven. I was in this club, something like an academy; I had a scholarship there. We had been busy drinking, drinking the whole night through, playing table tennis and drinking, and the next morning I had to walk out in the middle of a lecture and puke into the marigolds in the courtyard.

He was silent, listening to the sound of the word, marigolds; he seemed to have some kind of obsessive relationship with words; he examined the word, baring his teeth in the process. Then he continued. He said, I was thirsty. I was in urgent need of a glass of water; I had an unquenchable thirst for a big damn glass full of clear, ice-cold, wonderful water, and so I went into this bar. There was a bar; it belonged to the club, and the bartender wasn't there yet, but in spite of that there was a man sitting at the bar already. One man by himself. One man sitting alone at a bar in the bright, early morning, and I'm sure you know what I mean.

Samantha looked as if she were hearing this story for the very first time, which I found surprising. In the course of the evening her face had expanded, it had become brighter and more open. I thought I could see the girl she had once been and what she was like seven years earlier, back when Henry met her far away in the East and decided to try a second time. She had one elbow propped on the table and her head resting in her hand. She looked calm, relaxed, very much at one with herself.

He said that he was Neil Armstrong, Henry went on. He said he was the moon man, and I said something like, Oh, that's hard to believe. Ten o'clock in the morning, and what the hell are you doing here; what business brings you here? And he said that he was on a lecture tour, that he was on a tour to talk about the moon. To talk about what the moon had done to him. And I said, What did the moon do to you; and he said, The moon did me in. It really fucked me up. That's what he said.

Yup, Henry said. He stopped imitating himself; he gave that up. He raised his hands and let them drop to the tabletop. He said, That's it. That's what I wanted to tell you, that's all.

He thought it over a moment longer, and then he said, He was drinking Pink Gin. Back then. At that bar.

Ivo said, Pink Gin, what's that. He said it pleasantly, clueless, and something about this annoyed Henry; he wasn't prepared to explain. He said, shaking his head, Don't you know what Pink Gin is; I can't imagine that anyone here wouldn't know what Pink Gin is, and anyway, that's what Neil Armstrong was drinking, mixed it himself. He had raised his glass and said that I couldn't possibly imagine what it was like to stand on the moon and to see the Earth. To see this drop of water floating in the Universe, so alone and so fragile in the darkness. That I couldn't imagine how difficult it was for him to return to that Earth.

None of us said anything in reply. I wasn't sure whether

Henry had added the sentences about the return to Earth because Ivo had to ask his childish question about the Pink Gin; whether that part of the story wasn't actually entirely his alone. We were silent and twisted our empty glasses on the table and watched the drunken youngsters in the golden light up front at the bar taking off their shirts and embracing each other with their naked chests, holding each other.

We are dying, right, Henry said. That is a picture for dying, and as he said this, the tears came to his pixieish eyes, and he leaned far back in his chair.

Did you ever talk with anybody about it, Samantha said seriously. Did you tell anyone about it later when you came back to your room. That afternoon, the evening after that?

Of course not, Henry said. No one. I talked to nobody about it. That's how it was.

Later that night when I was walking home with Ivo, we stopped for a while on the swaying bridge. The swaying bridge crosses the river at a bend; it is attached with ropes; and when it's windy, it sways slightly. The bridge was on our way home; that was the only reason why we were standing at night in the middle of it and looking at the river; the moon was gone.

Ivo was silent; then he said, He thought that up himself. He cooked up this elegiacal story about the moon man; what was that all about. Armstrong after all died a hundred years ago, and besides, I know the story, I heard it before somewhere.

I said nothing. I thought, Either way, it's a good story,

and I thought I hadn't heard it before and it surely sounded true, and even if it wasn't, it still didn't change anything. Armstrong had told Henry that he had to leave a part of himself behind up there; that he was a ghost who would wander back and forth in his own footprints for all eternity; he was the Man in the Moon. And I thought that, from now on, so were we – Henry, because he had told us about it, and Samantha, Ivo and I because we had listened to him. But I couldn't talk to Ivo about this. I could only hold his hand, which was warm and somehow dry or chapped, as if a little bit of moon dust had been carefully passed on from Armstrong to Henry, and from Henry to Ivo, across all these years. I could only stand next to him on the swaying bridge and look across the river, searching the black water, scanning it for an improbable spark, a possibility.

Paper Airplanes

The interview is for late in the morning. Luke is still sick, and Sammy looks as if he were about to get sick. He's been awake since six o'clock, but in spite of that doesn't want to get up; his cheeks are hot and he's had his thumb in his mouth all morning long. Tess sits on the sofa with Luke, waiting for the digital beep of the thermometer under Luke's arm.

The longer you have to wait, the higher the fever, Luke says. His eyes are shiny and he shoves his hand under Tess's sweater as if he were actually still an infant.

Most of the time, Tess says. Not always. Let's see, 38.7. Not so good. Are you hungry, Luke? You're not necessarily feeling better, or are you?

Luke shakes his head dramatically.

Sammy says, Hungry. But Tess thinks he doesn't mean it. She can't leave the two of them alone, but she has to go; that's the predicament. So she phones Nick. It's early for Nick, and she lets it ring for quite a while, but then at some point he picks up. It's obvious that her call woke him.

She says, Nick.

He says, It's me.

She says, Can you come over for a couple of hours to stay with Luke and Sammy? They're both sick. Luke has a fever, and Sammy is coming down with one, and I have this interview; it's a good job, and I have the feeling I might get it. I have to be there at eleven o'clock. I have to leave the house at ten.

Nick says, Ten is in one hour.

He thinks that an hour is cutting it short. That it's hard for him to fully wake up, get dressed, have his coffee, tie his shoelaces, and get going in one hour.

Tess says nothing. She leans against the wall in the front hall and holds the phone to her ear and waits; it's not that she has to beg Nick; he's just slow; that's all, and she did, after all, wake him up. He always comes over when it concerns Luke and Sammy. He comes over even though Luke and Sammy aren't his sons. He would take care of Luke and Sammy every day if Tess wanted him to. If she would like him to. But she doesn't want that.

Nick says, OK. Give me a moment. I have to really wake up first. I'll be there at ten.

Tess says, Thanks.

She peels two pears and cuts them into small pieces. She makes tea for herself, milk with honey for Luke and Sammy. She takes the pears and the milk over to Sammy's bed. Luke is lying on his back next to his bed looking at something on the ceiling; Sammy still has his thumb in his mouth. They're listening to a children's tape, soft, high little voices singing something soothing.

Luke says, Well, I'm glad that I can stay home. That I can stay here with Sammy.

Sammy says, My Luke. My Mama. He doesn't take the thumb out of his mouth as he says it, but leans out of the bed and pulls Luke's hair.

Tess says, Your Luke and your Mama. She says, I'm going out soon and Nick is coming.

Luke says, Tell him to bring me something.

Tess says, I'll bring you both something.

She sits down next to Sammy on the edge of his bed and takes his little hot hand in hers. She sits that way for a while. When will you come again, whispers the voice in the cassette player, and another voice replies in a whisper, We'll come when we come. Tess thinks of a picture Nick once drew: Luke lying on his tummy in front of a collision of matchbox cars and Sammy on a little chair next to it, a prince with a green rabbit on his lap. Nick had been sketching casually; he'd simply drawn what he'd seen. Tess had kept the picture, but at the moment she doesn't remember where she put it, where it is. It's good for Luke and Sammy to spend time with Nick. Nick is calm and considerate, and he speaks to Luke and Sammy quite normally. Not like a

grown-up talking with a child. Not peevishly and hysteric-
ally like Tess sometimes.

Nick rings the doorbell at ten.

Tess is in the kitchen; she glances at the clock above the
stove; it says 10 o'clock and 26 seconds. She goes to open the
apartment door and stands by it watching as he comes up
the stairs, and she has to put her hands into the pockets of
her jeans to keep from embracing him.

In the hall she puts on a jacket; she says, Do you think I
should wear a hat. Is it cold outside. You could make something to eat around noon; there's soup in the refrigerator,
and both of them ought to drink some cherry juice; that
will bring the fever down.

Nick says, What sort of interview is it you're going to. You
should definitely wear a hat; it's freezing outside. Let me
guess. You certainly don't want to apply for a job at a bank.

This embarrasses Tess. She is wearing jeans and a decent
sweater, everything quite normal, just as usual, except she's
pinned her hair up so that she'll look older than she is. More
serious. A hat will ruin her hair-do. Never mind. She takes
a knitted hat off the coat rack and puts it on. She pulls the
hat down over both ears.

She says, At the welfare centre. At the crisis interven-
tion centre. The place for people who aren't doing too well.
People who are in a life crisis situation. Women who are
beaten by their husbands. Men who feel they have to beat
their wives when they're drunk. Problems like that.

It seems Nick doesn't want to go into more detail about this. He says only, Night shifts. Or what.

Tess says, Day shifts. Possibly a night shift now and then, sometimes a night shift, yes, but not regularly. Nothing bad. Nothing that would be dangerous, Nick. You're just supposed to be there, to talk with the people, watch out that they don't – go off the deep end, that they don't hurt themselves. You're supposed to listen to them. Nothing more. Don't look at me like that.

Actually Nick isn't even looking at her. He's just standing there. He still looks quite sleepy; on his right cheek there's a clear impression of his pillow, and he's combed his hair with water.

Tess says, What's the matter. What's wrong. Do you think it's not a good idea or something. Do you think I shouldn't go there. That someone like me shouldn't go there. Are you wondering what I'm going to tell them.

She starts shifting her weight from one foot to the other; she feels edgy.

Nick smiles; he says, No, that's not what I'm wondering. Of course you ought to go there. I'm sure you're good at that, watching that people don't go off the deep end. Don't hurt themselves.

Tess doesn't know how she's supposed to take that.

Do you really mean it.

And Nick says, I really mean it, Tess. Go ahead. Don't worry. Good luck!

It's already late afternoon by the time Tess gets back,

and she has a bad conscience. She's gone shopping: a loaf of white bread and honey and oranges, a beer for Nick and one for herself and chocolate ice cream for Luke and Sammy, a new comic book for Luke and a frog you can wind up for Sammy. She's tired. She comes home and puts the grocery bags down in the hall and goes to the bathroom; she washes her hands for a long time, her wrists and then again her hands and then her face before she takes off her jacket; before she goes into the living room.

Luke, in pyjamas with heavy socks on his feet, is sitting on the carpet folding paper. Sammy is lying behind him on the sofa; he is tearing paper; he says, My paper. Nick is sitting next to Sammy; he has his hands crossed behind his head; the imprint of the pillow on his cheek is gone. He doesn't say, How was it, Tess; and Tess is grateful to him for that.

She says, What did you do. How are you. How are you, Sammy; she sits down between Nick and Sammy on the sofa and puts a hand on Sammy's forehead, and he puts his little hand on top of her cool hand and holds it there.

We built paper airplanes, Luke says solemnly. For the world championship, right? He looks up at Nick questioningly. For this new record.

The record is at 29.2 seconds flight duration, Nick says. Takuo Toda in Japan; that was 19 December 2010. Or Tony Felch, United States of America; wait, that was a long time ago, I think 1985? Flight distance 58.8 metres. You have to fold the corners diagonally; the upper edge of the paper has to be exactly on the side edges. Then fold the upper edge of the paper down. The corners towards the middle – like this – and open them up again. You have to do it exactly like that.

Tess looks at them. She watches Luke as he, the tip of his tongue between his teeth, folds the paper; he bends it rather than folding it. She watches Nick, who is also folding, very neatly, carefully and precisely, as with everything else he starts. And he also finishes everything he starts.

She touches his shoulder. Stay for supper. Stay a little longer, Nick; I'll cook something for us, and there's a cold beer in the fridge.

Later Nick does ask. So, Tess. When do you start?

They'll call me, Tess says. They said they'd call in three days at the latest; they may want to agree on a trial period. They have to discuss it among themselves. We'll see.

Nick says, What did you tell them. He doesn't look at Tess; he looks down at the table while with his index finger he pushes together the wax he's scraped from the candlesticks.

The truth. I told them the truth, what else? I said that I have two children and that I'm their sole caretaker and that I have experience with psychiatric wards. That's how I phrased it. That I had been at home for a long time, and wanted to get out again now. To work. I said, I'm up to it; I have staying power, I'm optimistic. I have stability and inner calm. And I crossed my legs; drank coffee without milk or sugar, and didn't let my head wobble. Any more questions?

Any number, Nick says. I'd like to know how you felt there. I'd also like to know what kind of people work there in that ward; what the team is like, for example.

Tess thinks about it for a while. Then she says, Barbara and Christopher and Stan? Stan was OK. A guy who wears sandals with socks and pins postcards with mottos up over his computer and who looks as if he never sleeps. Barbara could be his older sister. Christopher is the boss. Pleasant. Domineering. Every gesture a warning; you know the sort of thing, Nick. The trick is to slip under his radar. Simply to duck, to act as if you accepted it. But in reality you're just slipping through under it. Know what I mean?

I do, Nick says. I know what you mean. And did you see any people? People in crisis. People with problems.

No, didn't see any, Tess says. They had shut them away or put them in restraints, or they simply didn't have any there just then.

She raises her hands and spreads the fingers, carefully putting her fingertips to her temples and pressing slightly. Then she lowers her hands again. She says, Sometimes I think I'd like to take everything apart and put it together again. Not to start all over again from scratch, that's not what I mean. But doing something else with what's there? Ah, well, that just wouldn't work. Look at Sammy and Luke. I don't think I can go back again.

What did it say on Stan's postcards, Nick says. They both have to laugh at that.

I don't remember any more. Something totally idiotic about a little snail, Tess says, climbing very, very slowly up

Mount Fuji? Nick, I wish I could tell you something different. Do you believe me.

That night they're all standing by the open window. Tess has Sammy in her arms; she's wrapped the blanket tightly around him. Luke has put on his anorak. Nick holds up the paper airplane; he says, If you throw it fast, if you throw it quickly you can overcome gravity for a moment. Three seconds gliding phase. Then it has to fly.

Luke says, Go.

Go, Sammy says.

The plane soars out over the street and on towards the railway tracks, towards the tall poplars. The tracks glimmer, and the white wings seem to dissolve in the darkness.

Islands

In the photograph we're sitting in front of a house that I can't remember. In any case it isn't Zach's house. On the left, that's me; Martha is sitting on the right. Oddly enough our posture is exactly the same, only in mirror image. Legs crossed, my left hand on my right arm, Martha's right hand on her left arm; this is probably because we used to spend a lot of time together. I remember the red dress I was wearing in the photo and the blue stone on Martha's necklace, not really a necklace in the usual sense, more like a rope. A cord. Whose were the dirty towels in the pile of laundry next to me; whose were the things on the wicker chair behind Martha, the shirts hanging on the clothesline above us? They weren't ours. I'd say the expression on my face is pleasant, a bit impatient. Martha looks sceptical. We obviously hadn't combed our hair for days; I'd totally forgotten that my hair had ever been that long. The plant growing into the picture on the right must be a banana tree. We're not wearing shoes. Whose house are we sitting in front of? And who took the photo; who saw us like that.

I occasionally run into Martha at birthday parties or the openings of exhibitions, at concerts; I haven't completely lost track of her. When we meet on an evening like that, we maintain a cautious distance, watching each other for quite a while – surreptitiously; we're getting older; in which ways and how … But then we do approach each other and start a conversation that's similar to the conversations we used to have with each other twenty years ago, and yet completely different.

Good evening, Iris.

Martha. Nice to see you.

Most of the time it's Martha who starts the conversation; it's easier for her, today as it was back then, easier for her than for me. It's not that she's entirely without inhibitions; at first her tone of voice is ironic and her body language quite formal; she looks as if she actually wanted to bow. But behind this, behind the formality, there's still this great fondness, a boundless warmth – almost irresistible for me. This lasts a little while. Ten minutes, a quarter of an hour – then we're talking together as if nothing had happened. As if almost nothing had happened. About mutual acquaintances, separations, weddings. Inevitably, about work. We talk about our children, Martha also has a daughter; both our children are doing poorly in school; their worst subject is maths.

How is that possible?

With such intelligent, exceptional mothers.

If we've had a lot to drink, and Martha still drinks too much – which probably won't change any more – we also talk about other things. About partings. Illnesses. About funerals. If Martha is completely drunk, she'll tell me, every time, that she can't help imagining that she's standing at my grave. She imagines I died and she had to go to my funeral, and as she describes this scene, she eventually bursts into tears. But still, that doesn't change anything. It changes nothing; we don't connect with each other any more.

Twenty years ago we lived together in America for a while. We had intended to emigrate, but came back to Europe; towards the end of our stay we had spent several weeks with a friend of Martha's in the Antilles – with Zach, and that's where this photo must have been taken. Zach lived in a dilapidated place in the hills, a one-storey building with a tower in the middle from which you could see across the entire jungle down to the bay. In that house I had a room next to the kitchen. Martha slept up in the lighthouse tower together with Zach. Later I sometimes thought that Martha had prostituted herself so that we could spend some time – would have time for each other. Swimming, driving around in the Jeep, drinking rum, picking mangoes, and lying in a hammock, smoking – so that we could do things like that. I'm not sure any more whether I merely thought this or possibly even said it aloud. But then Martha and Zach knew each other from the old days. Maybe that is all there was to it.

The house had a staff of two, a dark-skinned man and a dark-skinned woman.

Bumpy and Squeaky.

Martha and I couldn't get to the bottom of why they had these awful names, nor could we find out what their relationship to each other was. Brother and sister? Husband and wife? Cousins? We couldn't figure out their relationship to Zach either; Martha claimed Squeaky had moved out of Zach's room the day she moved in, that she had seen Squeaky carry her few belongings down the spiral staircase. Who knows. Clearly, things were happening behind the scenes. They were not what they seemed; the first night I lay sleepless on my back in my little room next to the kitchen – a room with a mattress under a mosquito net, a three-legged stool, and a turquoise-painted board on two sawhorses for a table – listening to the rustling and breathing outside my window; rustling and breathing that sounded as if it might have been almost anything. But the next morning it turned out that it was only wild dogs. Playful wild dogs in the wet grass.

And then there was the boy. A white boy, sixteen or seventeen years old. He could have been eighteen too, a delicate eighteen-year-old with fine, almost-white hair. Thin; he gave the impression of having experienced something really bad; he hardly ever spoke; sometimes he laughed at a joke, but his laugh was tinged with anxiety as if he actually knew better. He slept a lot. He slept all day on the sofa downstairs in the kitchen; he didn't wake up till evening.

He wasn't really a guest. But just what was he then?

I can't remember his name, and I'm sure Martha can't remember it either, that neither one of us can recall what his name was.

And after a while Zach drove off. Perhaps he dealt drugs or he had interests in drugs or other shady operations; he never said a word about how he actually financed the house, his employees, the three cars and the flights to Los Angeles. In any case, he drove off, intending to be away for some time, but before he said goodbye, he stocked the pantry and counted the gallon jugs of water and showed Martha how she could switch on the alarm system before she went to sleep in the evening up in the tower without him. It was as if he counted on being away for a while, but he didn't say anything about that. He didn't talk about it. He left the house at the crack of dawn, and that day, I remember exactly, it wouldn't stop raining, and Martha and I and Bumpy and Squeaky sat in the kitchen with the terrace door open, hour after hour, playing Pick-up-sticks while this constant, misty rain fell outside. The boy lay on the sofa and watched us. Bumpy was a fantastic Pick-up-sticks player. The best.

The policemen came at dusk. They came driving up the

meadow in two cars, which looked dramatic – the headlights in the twilight, the fine drizzle caught in the beams
of the headlights – and they all got out at the same time,
a detective in a shiny rain slicker and five police officers
with machine guns. They approached the terrace not in
any particular hurry, but very purposefully, and Martha
made an attempt to slide the terrace door closed; that's also
what Martha was like; she felt responsible. And of course
that was foolish; the detective was already standing on the
threshold, and he slid the door open again and said, We
have a warrant to search this house; and that's all he said.

I was sure they had no search warrant.

They searched the house. They separated us, pushing us
all into different rooms. The detective pushed me into my
little room with the mattress, the mosquito net, the three-
legged stool and the turquoise board, and he dumped the
contents of the metal box in which for some absurd reason
I'd collected and saved the things from my trip with Martha
out on the floor. He stamped on them with the toe of his
shoe – shells, barrettes, matchboxes; he stamped on them
the way you stamp out the glowing tip of a cigarette.

They took the boy away. They took Squeaky and Bumpy
too, but we got the impression that they'd let them out again
at the next street corner. Above all, they took the boy, and
he was wearing nothing except for a pair of white under-
pants as they pushed him into the car; he was bleeding and
holding his hands over his genitals, and that was the last we
saw of him.

Bumpy and Squeaky said nothing to us in parting. The detective got into the car, and then he got out again and came back to the terrace where Martha and I were standing, with the ravaged house behind us and the broken sticks from the Pick-up-sticks game; and he said that he wanted to point out to us that from now on we would be alone up here.

Totally and utterly alone and on our own; he wanted us to realise this; it was important to him. It mattered to him. He added that they would come again; that this was the only thing that he could say with certainty – they would be back.

And then? What would happen then.

What else still comes to mind when I look at that photo – Martha and me in front of a hut of weathered wood with a closed door and a dirty little window behind blinds made of straw – and who in the world had taken this photo; who saw us like this. It certainly wasn't Zach. I'm also reminded of the special way Martha would pronounce my name; her habit of always weaving my name into the sentences she said to me as if she really meant me or as if she wanted to show me how very seriously she meant me. But I'm afraid in the end I never reacted to it.

Yes – what happened then.

If you were to ask us that question today, on an evening like this – at a birthday party, a vernissage, a concert or a funeral; as we're leaning against a wall; each of us holding a glass of champagne, and both of us, independently of each other, prone to saying little, to silence, to long inward pauses in the conversation – if you were to ask us this question today, we couldn't give you an answer. I'm sure that Martha couldn't give you an answer either. Neither Martha nor I can remember what happened after that. We don't remember. Basically, we're standing there to the present day; we're still standing hand in hand and barefoot on the terrace of that house on the island, and night is already approaching in long strides over the beautiful blue mountains.

Poplar Pollen

Markovic kept the engine running as if his sister Bojana were robbing a bank. Selma was sitting in the back. It must have been winter; it was freezing cold, already dark, and stormy. Bojana came running across the car park, dropped into the passenger seat, and Markovic stepped on the gas even before she could pull the car door shut. He pointed back over his shoulder at Selma and said, That's my new girlfriend. Take a look at her; do you like her?

Bojana turned around to look at Selma; then she said, Striking.

They were simply picking Bojana up from work. Like that. That's how Selma first met Bojana.

Ten years later Selma and Markovic get divorced. Selma divorces Markovic. Could be she might remarry him, but for the time being she divorces him; right now she is exhausted. She'll have to see what's going to happen next. She is in her mid-forties; something in her life has to calm down. She herself has to calm down, and that's simply not possible as long as she's living with Markovic.

During the divorce proceedings, she avoids Bojana. Maybe she's afraid Bojana might try to make her change her mind. Perhaps seeing Bojana is painful because Bojana is married and staying married. She has been married to Robert for an unbelievable twenty-seven years. Selma, at the beginning of her own marriage, had said to Markovic, We'll be like your sister and her husband. She had visualised it like that. A long time ago. After the divorce she starts to meet with Bojana again. It takes a while; then she's ready. She loves Bojana; it's absurd to avoid her.

Bojana phones Selma and says, Why don't you come over. Come for a glass of wine.

Selma assumes that Markovic is far away on the days when Bojana phones her. That he won't just happen to drop in at Bojana's for a glass of wine too. She has actually never talked about this with Bojana; she believes that they have an unspoken agreement. There's a large table in the middle of the kitchen in the apartment in which Bojana and Robert have been living for twenty-five years; above the table there's a rotating mobile of the planets that Bojana's youngest daughter made. The balcony door opens out to the courtyard; old paper is piled up in one corner; the wooden floor is worn; on the wall hang colourful scribbles by Bojana's grandchildren, group photos from family birthdays, the horoscopes Bojana drew up for her daughters, their husbands and her daughters' girlfriends, for Robert and for Markovic. At the very beginning, more than ten years ago, there was also a joint horoscope for Selma and Markovic. A promising horoscope, a rosy future; Bojana had been surprised at the unusually favourable constellation, but she also had misgivings; she had expressed some warnings. Neither Selma nor Markovic thought it was worth talking about. They didn't pay any attention to it.

Robert lays the table. He sets out little wooden boards and wine glasses; puts out cheese, olives and bread. He's always the one who sets the table; his penchant for the wooden boards bothers Selma although she can't say why. Bojana keeps starting to do things, stops, and starts doing something else. She puts a bottle of wine on the table and says, I'm going to open a good bottle of wine for us. But then she puts the corkscrew down on top of the dishwasher and opens the refrigerator without taking anything out; and then she goes to get her cigarettes. Robert uncorks the wine.

Bojana says, It's quite obvious that you had to come over today, Selma. Couldn't be any other way, what with such a wonderful Venus in Pisces and Saturn in the Seventh House. Really quite obvious!

Robert is a sculptor. The centaur with two tails in front of the lilac hedge in the courtyard is his. He calls Bojana's astrological readings hocus-pocus. In spite of that he likes listening to them – apparently he likes the words, the world of images behind them, all these planets and transits, directions of the sun's arc, the radix, the idea of a seventh house. At first Robert was rather reserved vis-à-vis Selma; he had treated her, strictly speaking, as if she were a spy. Now it's different. Ever since she divorced Markovic it's been different.

He says, Sit down, Selma. Have something to eat. Eat and drink.

Bojana and Robert had been to Georgia together. They brought back dried pomegranates and Georgian brandy.

Bojana says, Robert and I drank this make of brandy in the hotel with a pimp and his whore.

And what was it you asked him, Robert says. He wants her to act it out; she's supposed to act out the way it was in the Georgian hotel. What exactly did you ask the pimp.

I asked the pimp about love, Bojana says with dignity. I said, What do you think of love?

And what was the pimp's answer, Robert says.

He said, I'll smack you in the kisser, Bojana says. That's what he said.

And then she laughs, uproariously, indignantly and delightedly all at the same time.

Good gracious, Robert says. Dear God in heaven. Just imagine it. How can anyone ask something like that, Selma. Be honest. Would this sort of thing have happened to you too? Would you be capable of asking something like that?

I'd certainly like to know what a pimp thinks about love, Selma says affably.

Well what is a pimp supposed to think about it, Robert says.

He pours more wine into their glasses and pushes the board with the cheese and olives towards Selma; he cuts some fresh, thick slices of bread. He shakes his head – how can anyone be so stupid.

He says, Well anyway, Bojana has bought herself a horse. Did you know about that? Has she already told you? That's the latest. She bought herself a horse and a piece of pasture-land, and she drives out to see the horse every day and feeds it apples and nuts.

And carrots, Bojana says. Apples, nuts and carrots, and I also add linseed oil; just imagine. The horse is incredibly beautiful. It's far too beautiful. The cars on the road stop, and people get out and call to the horse and pet it, and then they stuff it full of bad sugar. If I didn't feed it linseed oil and carrots, it would die. It would die miserably.

Can you ride it, Selma says. She has the feeling she ought to be saying something too for a change.

Well, not yet, Bojana says evasively. It's too young. It's still too young. At some point I'll ride it. In the future. Maybe.

The fact is, Robert says, it's not quite clear yet who is more afraid of whom. Bojana of the horse or the horse of Bojana. But that will change, right, Bojana? It will change. Once the Moon is in Pisces, then this will all be different.

And he strokes Bojana's hair with his large hand.

In the kitchen that evening towards midnight Robert notices there's a smell of burning.

Can you smell it? Oh well, Bojana, you can scarcely smell anything any more, but Selma, can you smell it; it definitely smells of smoke.

He's right, it does smell of smoke. Oddly enough Bojana and Selma aren't worried. They think nothing of it. Robert goes out into the hallway. The neighbours' doors open and slam shut again, and someone calls the fire department. Bojana leans over the balcony balustrade and says calmly, Well, the courtyard is already filled with smoke. Then she gets the Georgian brandy and two little glasses out of the cabinet, sits back down at the table, opens the bottle and pours some for Selma and some for herself.

Are we sitting in a burning house, Selma says.

We are indeed, Bojana says. So we are. We're sitting in a burning house. We're clinking glasses with each other in a burning house, and moreover we're doing it on principle.

They raise their glasses and drink, and then they kiss each other on both cheeks.

How is Markovic, Selma asks. The question escapes from her lips plain and simple; she can't take it back.

How's he doing.

Oh, Markovic, Bojana says. Markovic. How should he be doing?

In the end it was only poplar pollen. The white, fluffy, light snow of poplar sperm driven by the wind into a corner of the courtyard, driven behind the centaur with the two tails, spontaneous combustion. It happens sometimes, and that was all it was, nothing more. After the fire department had left, the kitchen smelled of damp soil, of smoke, and of summer.

As she was leaving Robert said to Selma, You've learned to set limits. With Markovic you've learned, once and for all, where your limit is.

He had been drunk and had embraced her in a way he hadn't done in all those years she was with Markovic, and Selma had gone home with that sentence, and the next morning it was the very first thing she remembered.

What kind of limit?

And why was it at once both comforting and terrible.

And all this happened quite a while ago. Several years ago. At some point Robert did leave Bojana after all; from one day to the next he filed for a divorce, and now it seems he's living with a woman who is five years older than Bojana, who favours net stockings and dyes her long hair henna red. That's what Selma has heard; she doesn't see Robert any more. She does see Bojana. Bojana goes out just about every evening to see her horse and standing shoulder to shoulder with the horse in the meadow, she holds her hand up to the soft horse's muzzle, and they walk along the path for a while and back again. Sometimes Selma drives out with her and watches. Bojana tells Selma that she doesn't know whether she'll ever have enough time to understand it all. To understand why Robert left her. With whom exactly she had been living almost her entire life, had spent more than half her life.

Sometimes Selma thinks back to that night with the poplar pollen. About the words, spontaneous combustion, about this term. She thinks, Love might be a form of spontaneous combustion, but that thought has no substance either, so she dismisses it.

Some Memories

Greta is lying on the chaise longue; she says she doesn't feel herself. Nothing bad, no pain, she simply doesn't feel herself.

She says, Tomorrow I'll get up again. Or, the day after tomorrow at the latest. Promise.

Maude says, I'll take you at your word. I'll call and remind you that you intended to get up again. An announcement.

Greta nods. Like a child, as if she believes what Maude says.

Maude says, In two days I'll be gone. Do you remember? I'm going away. The day after tomorrow I'm taking a plane to go on holiday.

Oh yes, Greta says. Where was it you were going?

To Lago d'Iseo, Maude says quite loud. To Italy, to Lago
d'Iseo.

Lago d'Iseo, aha, Greta says.

Maude has been living at Greta's for almost a year. She
never thought she would stay so long – to be honest, she
expected that living with Greta might be trying, but the
year is almost over and so far she hasn't thought about
looking for another room. Greta lives in a large house next
to the park. She is eighty-two years old, more than fifty
years older than Maude. She used to live with her family
in this big house, three floors and seven people – Greta,
her husband Albert and five children. Unimaginable, five
children, three of them from Albert's first marriage; two of
them Greta's own. There was a dog, and numerous cats.
Albert is dead. The children are gone. The dog is dead too;
of the cats one is left, a calico who is blind in the left eye.
Greta lives in the rooms on the ground floor. What used
to be the dining room is now her bedroom, but the living
room is still the living room; she has her own bath, rents
out two rooms on the first floor and also the attic room; the
kitchen is there for everyone, the garden too. The garden is
wonderful. Rambling and untamed, there are paths leading
to islands full of mullein and lupines; as a young woman
Greta always had a weakness for butterfly bushes and now
her butterfly bushes are dense as a forest.

Maude won't ever forget the introductory interview.
Greta was sitting in the kitchen, busy with gas and electricity bills, distracted, unfocused; she made a confused

impression on Maude. Gaunt and hunchbacked, her white hair cut short – clearly she had cut it herself – and her face looked masculine and serious, only the eyes had a lucid quality, blue and very light, and at first Maude had to avert her own when Greta looked at her. The kitchen was messy, not dirty, just untidy, and there was no way to tell whether that was Greta's or her housemates' fault. Greta had been going through her papers; her hands seemed huge to Maude, tanned a dark brown, spotted, with enlarged knuckles and wrists already curved inward.

Do you read books, Greta had asked her; she had asked without looking at Maude, casually and quite indifferent. Do you have any complicated psychopathological relationships that might lead me to expect that doors would be slammed here and you would be sitting at my kitchen table, crying. What kind of work do you do, do you work at all? Have you ever had anything to do with an old person? Do you take drugs. Do you do any sort of Far-Eastern meditation. Do you wash your hands before you eat supper? Do you like being alive? Do you value what you have? Do you cherish your Life?

Well, to be frank, I don't read all that much, Maude had answered. For a while I used to read detective novels, but that was a long time ago, and whenever anything gruesome happened in those books, I couldn't forget it; so I stopped reading them. I don't know what you mean by psychopathological; at the moment, anyway, I don't have a relationship and it's unlikely that I will have another one anytime soon, and you'll never find me sitting at your kitchen table crying.

I am a waitress. I didn't train to do that, but I can do it, and I work at the Mexican restaurant by the train station. I smoke marijuana. After I finish work, I roll myself a joint, and I smoke it before I go to sleep, and I'm sure you wouldn't forbid my doing that. The last old person I had anything to do with was my grandmother, but I was still a child then. Is an old person different in some way? I'm not at all involved in meditation. I wash my hands three times a day.

She had been sitting facing Greta with her arms crossed. She thought each of her answers had been wrong – above all, the one about the books – but Greta had looked up pleasantly from her bills and said, and Life? How about Life. You didn't answer my last question.

No idea, Maude had said. Don't know whether I like living, whether I value Life. Should I?

Well now, I don't know about that either, Greta had said with a smile so enigmatic and mysterious that Maude felt chills running down her spine. The room is 300 a month. You can go upstairs and look at it. Then come back down in fifteen minutes and tell me what you've decided. I'll wait here for you. By the way, if you intend to move in here, you don't have to look after me. Under no circumstances.

Maude had gone upstairs and stood in the middle of the room for fifteen minutes; it was large, bright and unfurnished except for a crooked tree branch suspended by two ropes from the ceiling that was perhaps supposed to serve as a clothes rod. There were seashells lying on the windowsill as if someone had forgotten them there, and a postcard wedged into the light switch showing a ship against a lemon-yellow sky. The windows were open, and Maude could hear the wind in the fir trees and the sound of bicycles on the earthen paths in the park as well as a soft clattering down in the kitchen. She had gone back downstairs and had said to Greta, I'd like to rent the room, and Greta had said, Wonderful, do!

That was a year ago. The Chilean student who lived under the roof went back to Chile, and the bookkeeper who had rented the room next to Maude for a while got married and moved with his wife to an apartment on the other side of the park. For two months now Maude has been alone in the house with Greta, and she has a feeling that Greta is not really looking for new tenants; no one has come by, and as far as she knows, Greta has not advertised the rooms. Maude likes being alone with Greta, but she also finds there is something disquieting about this situation, and now she is going away on a trip; Greta will remain in the house, and Maude sees this as a difficulty. She goes to visit Greta around noon – that's what she calls it, visiting Greta; it means that she knocks on Greta's living room door or, in the summer, goes out on the terrace in order to sit with Greta for an hour or two. Maude likes Greta's living room. An enchanted room, plants clustered at the terrace door, full of things, untidy – the untidiness in the kitchen was Greta's untidiness; it hadn't taken Maude long to discover this – a room like a cave. Shelves line all the walls, and the books stand on them not simply in one row, but sometimes two, sometimes three rows deep. They're piled up in corners, on the table and around the chaise longue. Sometimes Greta picks out books to give away, but then she can't part with them. She told Maude that it was possible to read between four and five thousand books in a lifetime. Four thousand to five thousand – for Maude this is an inconceivably large number. She asked Greta whether she had read all the books in the living room, and Greta had answered gloomily, Not even a fraction; she repeated it, Not even a fraction. In the beginning Maude sometimes read aloud to her. It had just come about. On Greta's instruction she had stepped over to the bookshelf and with her eyes shut had picked a book at random from the many there and read one paragraph from it, and it was quite obvious that Greta knew every single book; her reactions went from being delighted to disgusted. In the evenings when Maude, having smoked her joint in the garden went, slightly stoned, to Greta in her room, it seemed to her as if the room, the books and Greta were part of a common structure, like a web, a latticework made of a material for which there was no name. But recently Greta had declined being read to. It's getting on my nerves, she said. This is gradually but clearly getting to be much too much for my nerves, and Maude had stopped in front of the bookshelves as if before a fissure in a rock that was closing.

From all the pages she had read aloud, she had chosen two sentences to memorise; she had learned the two sentences by heart. The sentence: 'Memory sheds the echoes of songs and of passions until nothing remains,' and the sentence, 'In the end the little white kid runs away from us and we become orphans.' Greta said that the first sentence surely didn't apply to Maude but rather to herself, to Greta. Maude said, Well, neither one applies to me. I just find them beautiful. I like little white kids. These are beautiful sentences; do you know what I mean? And sad sentences, Greta had added, and Maude had agreed. Yes, and sad sentences too. OK.

She knocks on the living room door, a sliding door with leaded stained-glass panes; she can't really make out anything through the vine tendrils and grapes. It takes a moment until Greta answers her knock; Maude slides the door open with a pounding heart. It's true, she doesn't have to take care of Greta, but that doesn't change the fact that she thinks about Greta.

Greta is lying on the chaise longue. Just like yesterday – yesterday she had also lain there and hadn't got up. Hanging on the wall behind the chaise longue is a tapestry on which helmeted warriors with lances are gathering; the small table is overflowing with newspapers, documents, old letters: correspondence, that's what Greta calls it, my correspondence. She always has to be careful not to put the newspaper on top of the ashtray with her burning cigar. Greta stacks the empty cigar boxes in which she collects scraps of paper and newspaper clippings into towers; she writes key words on scraps of paper that she leaves lying around everywhere. Sometimes she asks Maude; she says, Maude, do you know why I wrote that down? Glacier milk. Why did I want to remember that? And she mumbles to herself and shakes her head, saying, Glacier milk, glacier milk.

Maude stands by the chaise longue, hands on hips. She looks at Greta; at other times Greta would return her gaze; she often senses when Maude is depressed, and she can also tell when Maude is truly happy, and sometimes she says something about it. But today she doesn't seem to be in the mood to say anything at all. She is lying on her back, her large hands folded on her stomach, looking at the ceiling. The cat is lying at her side. Greta says dully, What does the Mexican make. Tacos and burritos. Are you finished at work, or did they fire you. Excuse my mood, but I don't feel myself. I don't feel well today either, that's all.

I'll make us some coffee, Maude says. I'll make some coffee that will wake the dead, along with a quark and jam sandwich.

The dead can go to hell, Greta says, but she does make an effort; sits up, and starts looking for her glasses on the table.

Maude brews the coffee and prepares a sandwich for Greta and one for herself. Coming back to the living room with a tray, she puts it on the chair next to the chaise longue and says, Shall I open the terrace door, and Greta nods in agreement or simply absent-mindedly. Maude slides the door wide open and the cat bounds to the floor, brushes past her legs and soundlessly leaves the house. They both look out into the garden for quite a while without saying a word, almost in surprise at so much sunlight on the still-bare trees. Spring. The cool air coming into the room smells of fresh-mown grass.

I remember Lago d'Iseo, Greta finally says. Lago d'Iseo, that's where you're going, right? I was there once too.

Yes? Maude says. She turns to Greta. When was that? Have a little sip of coffee, for my sake; I made it Mexican style – added a little nutmeg and a teaspoon of cocoa. When were you at Lago d'Iseo.

A long time ago, Greta says. Fifty years? Even longer? I was about the same age as you are now. It's an impressive landscape; the mountains around the lake are impressive. Quite magnificent. But also morbid. Not my kind of landscape actually. Not at all my kind of landscape.

She lifts the cup off the saucer and blows into it. She's wearing one of her linen shirts and her bangles, several narrow silver bangles; for some reason Maude finds it reassuring that Greta put the bangles on that morning. She takes a tiny sip. She says, The nutmeg in the coffee is a good idea; then she puts the cup down again.

I've never been there, Maude says. I just thought that one could go swimming there. It will be hot, I'd like to swim and lie in the sun and drink Campari; that's all I want.

I went swimming, Greta says. Suddenly she looks as if she had a slight fever, flushed and pale at the same time. I went swimming just the way you'll go swimming. I sunned myself and drank Campari and read. The water there is wonderful, ice cold, dark blue; the lake is very, very deep. Pebbly beach. Really, so much time has passed, but I remember the beach and some of the names. Riva di Solto. Lovere, Paratico. There was an accident, I remember that too.

An accident, Maude says. She pulls a chair over to the table and sits down. She drinks some of her coffee and eats her sandwich, and then she eats the sandwich she made for Greta; she is sure that Greta won't eat it. The warriors on the tapestry stand behind Greta like her followers. Stand behind Greta like ancestors. Greta looks past Maude, so she says it again, An accident?

A swimming accident, Greta says. Is that what you call it? I had a green-and-red-striped towel. A deck chair close to the water. There was a family standing in the water. You'll see that too; that certainly hasn't changed; these Italians don't really swim. They stand around in the water; they stand in the water and talk. Grown-ups and children. One of the children had a boat, a little boat made of wood, a very fine boat with a white sail. The boat sailed off. I saw it sail off. Maybe I should have told them. Called their attention to it.

Greta says, I shouldn't be telling the story. Shouldn't talk about it.

Nonsense, Maude says. I'm not such a softie. What happened next?

Greta says, The boat sailed off. It sailed away, and they saw it too late; it was already too far out when they saw it. The little boy started to cry. And his father swam after the boat, an athletic man and strong, confident swimmer's strokes; for quite a while things looked all right. But that lake is treacherous. There are currents, whirlpools, ice-cold spots. Who knew that.

And then …, Maude says hesitantly.

He didn't come back, Greta says. I wasn't watching the entire time. What was I doing – I was reading, sleeping, I was sunning myself. But when I looked back again, he still hadn't come back, and the entire family was in a state – how should I say it. In a state of hysteria. Two carabinieri came along the beach. How odd they looked, their uniforms, their black official severity among all the bathers.

It seemed, Maude thinks, as if Greta had reached back into her memory. Her past. Or as if she were shedding her memories? Like leaves, like a skin.

Maude looks at Greta; there's a question on the tip of her tongue.

Did you know him? The athletic man who swam after the boat, the little boy's father. Did you know each other? Why didn't you say anything when you saw the boat sailing away.

But she doesn't ask. No, she doesn't ask.

Yes, Greta says. That's the way it was. But this certainly won't happen to you at Lago d'Iseo. You won't swim so far out, Maude. You'll be careful.

Shall I bring you your cardigan, Maude says.

That would be very kind, Greta says distractedly.

Maude goes to fetch Greta's cardigan from the bedroom. She glances at the photographs hanging over the bed – photos of Greta's husband, the children, the dog and the house, Greta's entire long life at a glance. Too little time. Too little time to discover Greta. Greta's expression half a century ago. Coming back to the living room, she puts the cardigan over Greta's shoulders, and she senses her touch isn't unpleasant for Greta, hasn't yet become alien to her.

She says, I have to go out again. I have to buy some odds and ends, and I have to pack my suitcase. I'll be away for two weeks; I don't think I told you that before. In two weeks I'll be back again.

She says, Will you be able to cope? You'll be able to manage by yourself like this, yes?

Hail to you, beautiful bay in which my youth came into bloom, Greta says.

She says, One really remembers the strangest things, from one moment to the next. Beautiful bay where my youthful dreams awakened. Of course I'll be able to cope by myself. Don't worry. Have a good trip, Maude. Take care.

Brain

Philip and Deborah have been trying for several years to have a child; by the time they give up, Philip is already fifty years old. He'd like to just drop the subject – he feels he could live out his life perfectly sensibly without a child. He is a successful photographer; there are still some things in this world he would like to photograph, things he'd like to put his mind to; it's not as if new ideas weren't occurring to him any more. But Deborah sees things differently. Deborah feels that she can't be happy without a child; she feels a terrible incompleteness, as if, without a child, a very crucial portion of knowledge would be denied her once and for all.

That is how she expresses it.

She keeps repeating it over and over again. She says, I feel as if I can't breathe any more without a child, and Philip can't think of anything to say in reply.

So, they agree to adopt.

Back then they were married and well off. Deborah had brought money to their marriage; she hails from prosperous circumstances. Money is not the problem. The problem is Philip's age; actually, he is too old to adopt a child. Deborah is exactly the right age; she is thirty-five, but Philip is a good ten years more, and only after some research does Deborah find an agency that also places children with old, with older parents – exclusively children from Russia. This agency doesn't care at all about the age of the parents.

Philip and Deborah spend a weekend at the agency. They sit together in a circle with seven other couples and talk about themselves, attempting to say something about themselves; they are supposed to try to be open. They listen to one another; it is astounding and also touching, how similar they are to one another; their modest needs, the simple longing for a family.

I long to get to this point, Deborah says. I have a longing for a table set for three.

Philip, sitting next to her, watches as she searches for words, wringing her hands, twisting her wedding ring – a woman in a state of extreme distress. But the sentences she then decides on are the exact opposite of the complicated theories she normally favours, her often-fatal weakness for on-the-one-hand-and-on-the-other; here there seems to be just the one hand. Deborah is facing away from him, her knees drawn up to her chest and her eyes fixed on the floor; she is surprisingly and totally alien to him. She is barefoot; he looks closely at her bare feet. He hears the way in which she pronounces the word 'longing', how she draws it out. He imagines a table set for three. The light on the table, falling on the table from the side, the blinding whiteness of the tablecloth.

The agency's residential meeting centre is located in the mountains. In the morning when Philip steps out on the terrace he doesn't know for one dizzying moment why they are really here. The smell of pine trees, snow on the mountaintops. What are they doing here? Deborah behind him in the shadowy room lying in bed, her hair spread out on the pillow like a fan. Then he remembers.

Sunday afternoon, the agency representative invites them to come to the conference room, just the two of them. The other couples are gone, have left, or they never really existed, just a sham, an arrangement of mirrors to allow the couple Philip and Deborah to become visible. To let everything come out into the open, especially those things they want to conceal.

The conference room is empty. The mats on which they had sat in a circle and were supposed to talk about themselves have been neatly piled up in a corner. The agent asks them to sit down at the table that is now in the middle of the room; he sits down across from them, puts a portfolio on the table, opens it, leafs through it searching, hesitating at one spot, turning back a page then forward again. He pauses one very last moment, then he turns the portfolio around and places it in front of Philip and Deborah, precisely between them.

He says, Alexej. As if there were only this one choice, no other.

In a shiny plastic cover, the photo of a child, perhaps two years old, below it a few details about his origin and adoption history.

Why Alexej, Philip says. Why this child. He senses that this is a question Deborah would never have asked. She already knows. This is her child.

The agency representative says, Because of the look in his eyes.

Deborah says nothing. She looks at the picture of the child, bends down close to examine it.

Philip and Deborah fly to Russia. Philip has been in Russia several times before, Deborah never. It doesn't seem to matter in the slightest to her that they are flying to Russia; since the weekend in the mountains, since the decision for Alexej, she has turned oddly silent, and sometimes Philip thinks of it as brooding, an image he would rather avoid. They fly to Moscow and from Moscow they proceed by bus; outside the city a broad, dark plain stretches to the horizon. In N. they take a hotel room in which you can neither turn off the heat nor open the windows. The orphanage is at the edge of the city; a Soviet-style building in an overgrown birch forest. For an hour they wait in a room that has seven chairs standing next to each other against a wall painted red; then the door opens and someone pushes Alexej into the room. He looks paler and thinner than in the photo. He looks stunted. He immediately goes to stand in a corner of the room and refuses to come out of it.

Come here, Deborah says. Come, come out; I won't hurt you. Sitting on her chair by the wall she leans forward and tries to entice the child as if he were a kitten; she is crying as she cajoles him. The child stands in the corner, not moving. He stares at them.

At supper they eat in the empty, spooky hotel dining room; they eat green salad with hard-boiled eggs and ice-cold peas and drink a sweet red wine that immediately goes to Philip's head. The waitresses stand in a row like soldiers; they stand there motionless, hands folded over their aprons; outside snow is falling in fantastic, fat flakes.

The peas are very good, Deborah says. The wine is a bit strange, don't you think; it's pretty sweet. But I think it's good. I'm OK with everything.

Besides them there's no one else eating supper in the hotel, and they take what's left of the wine back to their hot room. They phone their families. Philip phones his brother Joseph who sells cars and is the father of three children; the feeling of a family bond – his brother's voice, the barking of the golden retriever in the background, the noise of the television and the children fighting; Philips's sister-in-law calling them for supper, then someone ringing the doorbell – is absolutely overpowering. Where are you, Joseph calls into the telephone. Philip! The connection is terrible; I can't understand you. Call me again later! All the best!

Deborah calls her sister who lives in Hawaii and is a teacher. She leans her back against Philip's back while she's talking; Philip feels the vibration of her voice in his spine. She says, I don't know; maybe he's autistic. He seems so odd to me, motionless and silent; he doesn't talk; he just stares at us; can we risk it. Can we do this.

Deborah's sister seems to be saying something reassuring, to know a way of giving some comfort.

On the second day Alexej takes a hesitant step out of the corner. He clings to the wall, keeps his hands on the wall; he says nothing but turns around to Deborah three times. Philip, having thought long and hard about it, finally took his camera. He photographs the visitors' room. The view from the window. Deborah on the chair, her hands reaching out to the child; she is wearing a sweater made of brown, fluffy wool, and all the colours in the room turn darker from the outside towards the inside.

He also photographs the child's back, his soft, fragile neck.

On the third day Alexej comes towards them already in the entrance hall of the orphanage; Philip suspects that someone may have had a serious talk with him. He's wearing an anorak that's much too big for him, and he reaches for

Deborah's hand in a calm and definitive way. The three of them take a short walk in the garden. They walk around the birches and look at their tracks in the freshly fallen snow, two big sets and between them one small set.

We'll take him, Philip says that evening to the director of the orphanage; we are quite certain; we want to take him. The silent manner in which the director adds this information to the files seems right to him, appropriate.

That evening in their hotel room Deborah blows up several balloons. She had bought the balloons back home and taken them along to Russia; that had been her preparation. Red, yellow and blue, round and heart-shaped balloons; she leaves them lying around in the room, and during the night they keep bumping against each other in the hot drafts from the radiator. The next morning they pick Alexej up from the orphanage, and he walks out with them and between them without once turning around. Later they have the impression that this is the first time in his life that he has ever seen a balloon. He is delighted, totally enraptured.

One year later Philip begins working again. He has stayed home for all of twelve months; each and every day was spent taking care of the child together with Deborah; the child has adapted, he's doing well; Philip feels he can start working again, and it's high time. He rents a new studio and starts a new series; he has always had a great interest in surgical medicine, and he starts photographing in operating rooms; first during heart surgery, then during brain surgery. He photographs the delicate, highly specialised technological surgical instruments, silvery robots behind shimmering plastic sheets that seem to him like poetical images in the bluish light of the operating room, like deep-sea creatures. He photographs this for quite a while, for several weeks, and finally, at the end of the series, he photographs an operation on an exposed brain.

He talks about this photo with Deborah that evening at the table in the kitchen. He tells her about the arrangement of the machines, the surgeons' conversations during the operation, which of course were not about essentials, but rather strictly extraneous things, the exact opposite of the operation – tickets for the opera, the weather forecast, golf trips. In the past he used to talk a good deal about his work with Deborah, but since the child has been with them they've had little time for such conversations, and Philip thinks that he misses this; he misses Deborah's former predilection to want to see things from all sides. The child, whom they renamed Aaron – the name Alexej was too harsh for them, the x in the middle of the name too hard – is sitting with them; he is supposed to be eating his supper, and he is listening to them.

What sort of person was it on whose brain they were operating. Whose brain you photographed today, Deborah says as she looks at the child eating, watching him as he eats, again and again pointing to the cut-up tomatoes, the butterfly pasta; how is that person doing now. After the operation. What will happen from now on.

A woman, Philip says. The person whose brain I photographed was a woman. I photographed a female brain. I
discussed it with the doctors first, and she agreed to it. I
assume she's doing well.

Deborah waits for the child to swallow. She wipes the
child's mouth; she praises him.

Philip hesitates, then he says, If I had known what kind
of person lived with this brain, how she would do after the
operation, I wouldn't have been able to photograph it.

He watches as Deborah hands the child a glass of water,
and he sees from the look she gives him while the child
is drinking that they have arrived at a demarcation line, a
fork in the road where, surprisingly enough, he will again
be compelled to make a decision. Even though he has told
the truth. In spite of having told the truth. Precisely because
he did.

The child drinks all the water in the glass and puts the
glass back on the table by himself, carefully. Not looking
at anyone.

A Letter

For Helmut Frielinghaus

On the way back I spent a few days in Boston. I like being in Boston, and I also wanted to visit my friend, Walter, who like me comes from C., and his wife. Walter's father was Jewish, but they got out of Germany in 1939 or 1940, just in time. Our parents were friends and as a little boy I often played with Walter; he had, I remember clearly, a large model train set up in his cellar. Locomotives and express trains, tracks that led through papier-mâché mountains; the mountains were dusted with snow and in the ravines there were tiny fir trees. There were crossings and signals, a train station, a conductor and an engineer, baggage cars, figures waving on the platform, and suitcases and hatboxes the size of rice grains.

Walter is an eye doctor. He *was* an eye doctor, occasionally he still sees patients he has known for a very long time. He writes – big fat novels told at a rambling and leisurely pace in German, and he engages in extensive correspondence on his computer. He maintains his command of German by reading old German literature. He never reads anything new, or anything American, even though he speaks English fluently; after all, he grew up in America and studied at Harvard. He quotes Hölderlin, Goethe, Kleist and Rilke by heart in German, carefully and correctly, with a flat American accent – *dies ist ein Ding, das keiner voll aussinnt, und viel zu grauenvoll, als dass man klage: dass alles dauert und vorüberrinnt. (This is something really quite unbearable for anyone to fully imagine, and much too ghastly for one to complain: that everything lasts for a time and then passes.)*

These days Walter is actually a crazy man. A highly intelligent screwball, a philosopher, an eccentric. Still a good doctor; sometimes he gives me advice, he advises me about eye diseases, and he originated the sentence: An eye is as fragile as a Ming vase; I've adopted this concept for the entire body. He is an excellent technician. In the last few years he has built a three-storey annex to his house in Belmont near Boston, an annex with baths, heating and all the frills; he does almost all of it himself with the help of instructional manuals. And he has a project for his old age – a wooden house on Nantucket. The shell of the wooden house on Nantucket is complete, but for months now work on the house has had to be postponed because the authorities on the island won't grant approval for the use of his self-designed and self-built sewage treatment setup. He is taking them to court. He says he would continue with the legal proceedings until his death and even beyond.

During the time I was visiting Walter and his wife in Boston, we talked about the house on Nantucket, and I said if I ever came again I'd like to see it.

And he said, Shall we drive there tomorrow?

He said, Shall we drive there tomorrow, as if he assumed that I wouldn't be coming again, or as if he assumed that he wouldn't be around any more when I came again.

He asked Edna.

He said, Edna, shall we drive to Nantucket tomorrow, the three of us? Go on a little excursion. What do you think.

Edna is eighty-six years old. She is a quiet woman, a lover of wild flowers; she must have a rich and private inner life, and most of the time she is occupied with mysterious nota-tions that I would much rather read than Walter's novels. When Walter asked her whether we should drive to Nan-tucket together, she looked at us in silence, then she closed the botanical encyclopaedia in which she had just been looking up a branch that she had brought back from her daily walk; she got up and began to pack her rucksack.

They picked me up at six o'clock the following morning at my hotel. The hotel wasn't serving breakfast yet, and none of the staff were in sight, but there was fresh coffee along with a bowl of green apples on a table in the lobby. So I had a cup of coffee and ate an apple while I was waiting for Edna and Walter, reminded of other trips fifty years ago, of early departures at dawn, of the cold, of fading stars in a sky just beginning to turn light.

We drove to Cape Cod, to Hyannis; in Hyannis we parked the car and got on the boat to Nantucket. The trip took two hours, and we spent the time up on deck. From Nantucket Harbor we took a taxi to Walter's house. It is situated on a hill, and from the outside it looks like all the other houses on the island; it's a simple house of grey-stained wood. It has a cellar and two floors above that and sits on a large parcel of land covered with nothing but low-growing, creeping vegetation. Walter has two surveillance cameras, one in the house and one outside that is trained on the house, and both are connected with his computer in such a way that with the help of the internet he can check from Boston or any other conceivable place in the world to make sure that all is well; later I saw us on the videotape – Edna, Walter and me – entering the house, in the entrance hall, on the roof and on the terrace: our figures, our unsure but natural movements.

Edna, setting down her rucksack, taking something small out of it, and putting it in a corner of the room.

We had four hours to spend in the house on Nantucket before the taxi would pick us up again and the last boat left the harbour to return to Hyannis. During those four hours we mostly stood around one or the other of the two radiators; it was a bitterly cold day, windy and frosty, and the winter sun seemed only to intensify the cold. I walked swiftly through the garden several times to warm up. The walls inside the house were still missing; there was only the framing to show where they were supposed to be, and Walter led us through the rooms and furnished them out of the blue with beds and chairs, shelves and sofas, desks and carpets; he did this forcefully and believably. From the upper windows we could look out over a row of houses and down to the beach and the sea. We saw the surf; we could hear the breakers. We held our hands to the radiators, ate doughnuts from a cardboard box and drank hot tea from the thermos, all three of us from the same cup. During those four hours, Edna's face had a strange expression of contentment, at once glowing and secretive.

On the boat trip back she went below deck. I stood with Walter at the bow. The sun went down; the water turned silver, then blue, and then black. Nantucket stayed behind. Walter said that in the language of the Indians the name of the island actually meant 'the far distant land'.

From Hyannis we drove in the car back to Boston. We said goodbye in the hotel car park; I seem to recall that Walter and I embraced. At half past nine I was back in my room. Half frozen and strangely cheerful, I changed my clothes and went downstairs again to the bar to get something hot to eat and, above all, to have a drink.

I ordered a whiskey.

And then another.

This actually isn't my best time.

But I survived it all. I went back to New York and still had twenty-four hours to spend there, hours that were pleasant even though I didn't do anything special. I walked around, looked at the people, the streets, until I went to the airport in the afternoon and flew home.

Dreams

I liked him, and I think he liked me pretty well too. Effi
had just dropped this sentence, lightly and in passing, but
with a meaningful half-smile and a look that neatly passed
right over Teresa. Just as if she had fully understood the
lesson of her psychoanalysis, as if she had learned it all. She
said it conclusively, there was nothing more to add, and
with this assessment the positions were clearly assigned.

Back then Effi had had a mysterious appointment three
times a week; for two years she had talked about having
these appointments. And at the end of those two years,
during which she separated from the man to whom she'd
been married for an eternity and married another, she had
confessed to Teresa that the appointments had been for

psychoanalysis sessions. Not really a confession – she had simply cleared up the mystery, and at the end she said, By the way, I can recommend him to you. Doctor Gupta. I mean, if you're ever feeling bad, having a really lousy time of it, I mean if you simply don't know how to go on. I can recommend him to you.

By this time Effi's psychoanalysis was over and she was pregnant. As if Doctor Gupta had pulled off this feat, as if Effi's child were a creation of the mind.

During those two years when Effi had her appointment three times a week, the two of them would sometimes meet around noon for a cup of tea. They would meet in a café called the Yuri Gagarin; in the winter they sat inside; in spring and summer and also during the long autumn they sat outside. The chairs at the Yuri Gagarin had red seat covers, and dusty sparrows darted around the tables; they fed them the cookies served with the tea. Invariably Teresa found that the tea wasn't hot enough.

The hours at the Yuri Gagarin were above all polite and characterised by an amiable distance, as if they were each trying to leave the other alone or as if, on the whole, they were not really much interested in each other. They talked about books they'd read or hadn't read, about exhibitions, about this or that film. Effi had a trying habit of retelling films in their entirety; it would never have occurred to Teresa to interrupt her. Then shortly before one o'clock Effi would pay for her tea and set off to her appointment, which Teresa for some time suspected was with a lover, maybe one who wrote letters, a rather corpulent, bearded Arab with soft hands whose kitchen smelled of fresh mint. Unfortunately, there was no lover. Effi merely spent that time in the apartment of Doctor Gupta, whose practice was just around the corner and on whose couch Teresa too would be lying one year later.

At one of those midday meetings at the Yuri Gagarin, Effi told Teresa about a dream she'd had. Teresa didn't know the first thing about the interpretation of dreams; she listened to Effi; she understood what she heard; she would have said, I simply understood what I wanted to understand.

I dreamed about you last night, Effi said. I dreamed that we were both on a tram; we get on together and have to buy a ticket; we're standing next to each other at the ticket dispenser and suddenly you get very small. You shrink, get smaller and smaller, until you're really tiny, a dwarf.

She indicated Teresa's diminutive size with her hand, using thumb and forefinger, half a centimetre. She said, And then I pick you up. I pick you up and put you into my coat pocket.

Effi had a round face, expressive green eyes, slightly Asiatic features; her teeth were crooked, and she smiled one-sidedly, smiling only with the right side of her mouth, which always gave the smile an involuntarily sarcastic expression. Or was it voluntary? Teresa looked at Effi for a while. Then she thought, Effi dreamed that she was protecting me. Because she assumed that I'm actually tiny, tiny and small, and as fragile as an egg.

But some time after that Teresa felt so bad that she didn't know how to keep going. In Effi's words she was having 'a really lousy time'. She could no longer read the newspapers; she broke out in tears when she heard the traffic reports; and the growing hordes of refugees, catastrophes at sea, earthquake victims, forecasts of droughts, climate summits, plagues and massacres caused her to feel an irrational anxiety that got worse with each passing day. She developed a severe, itchy rash on the inside of her elbows, on her neck and on her face. She couldn't stand the sound of ambulance sirens, the radio and the newscasts any more, she would wake up at three o'clock at night with a racing heart and have great difficulty going back to sleep, and she could scarcely move because of an overwhelming feeling of grief. On dozing off she dreamed of missed appointments, elevator shafts and slugs. And one morning when she started to cry before it was even light outside, she phoned Doctor Gupta. She went to see him in his office for the first time on a November afternoon, and she pushed a piece of paper across his desk that she had prepared at home; she had managed to write no more than the one sentence: Somehow I don't know how to go on from here.

But that was long ago. Years ago. By now Teresa has been going to Doctor Gupta for years. She hasn't gotten pregnant. She has survived numerous separations – among them her separation from Effi; she simply broke off her idiotic relationship with Effi. But the relationship with Doctor Gupta continues; it remains intact. During those years Doctor

Gupta has moved his office four times. He moved from the office near the Café Yuri Gagarin into a communal practice where there were people sitting in the crowded waiting room who obviously had more serious problems than Teresa. For a few months he moved his office to a carriage house in a shaded, damp and chilly rear courtyard, and then he moved into a medical office building at an intersection that was so noisy that a timidly spoken word could barely be understood. For some time now he has managed to hold out in an attic apartment, in a consulting room from which Teresa, lying on his couch, can see the wide sky and birds gathering in great flocks; she can see satellite towns, factory chimneys and windmills far away on the horizon.

Doctor Gupta practises classic psychoanalysis. He sits behind Teresa in an armchair; she cannot see him while she is talking or not talking. The office furnishings have remained the same through all the moves; the couch is the same couch Effi used to lie on, the enigmatic painting of a hot air balloon above a ridge of hills is the same; the bookshelves contain only professional literature; there is always a carefully chosen flower arrangement in a floor vase next to his desk. The curtains are cream-coloured. The carpet, an oriental, the blanket on the couch, also oriental. Doctor Gupta's armchair is shabby, especially the headrest. Sometimes he puts a personal book on his desk like a lead. A clue, a mysterious hint: *Oblomov.* Julia Kristeva's *Tales of Love,* short stories by Capote. Teresa picks up on these hints. She collects them, keeps them, and thinks about them, occupying herself with them in a way that is insistent and in spite of that strangely uninvolved. Perhaps it's similar in nature to the way Doctor Gupta listens to her, following her long-winded, always identical, clueless circling around a central point. Or not following – there are hours when she is certain that she can tell from his breathing that he is asleep. She thinks, Just turn around. Sit up and look at him; catch him sleeping dammit.

But she doesn't sit up, she doesn't turn around.

At home she puts the same flowers next to her desk, moves her couch over to the window, and reads Julia Kristeva. Doctor Gupta has revealed to her in which section of the city he lives, and she knows that he has a passion for the English language; when he uses English diagnostic terms, his voice trembles with emotion. He plays classical guitar; some days the guitar stands in a corner of the room; the fingernails of his right hand are long and manicured. He is fat and sad, a massive man with a shaved skull, carefully polished shoes and a penchant for unusual, extravagant shirts and expensive trousers. One entire summer he wore a cork on a piece of string around his neck that looked as if it were supposed to remind him of something important.

Is he homosexual?

Married?

Why does he keep moving all the time.

Does he have children?

He has no children; Teresa knows, although she doesn't know how she knows, yet she knows for certain.

But once when he opened the door for her, he had a black

eye. A black eye; his right eye was impressively discoloured: blue, green, dark violet and black.

Oh, Teresa said. Who started it. Did you hit first? Or were you defending yourself; did you by chance hit back.

I hit back, Doctor Gupta said, surprisingly candid. He emphasised each single syllable – I hit back.

He smiled; there was no more to say.

At another of her sessions Teresa happened to think of the Café Yuri Gagarin, of Effi, of her dream, the dream Effi had dreamed back then. With the years, Teresa has been dreaming less and less; her dreams are blurry and she remembers them only vaguely, and she thinks that Doctor Gupta is probably disappointed in her because of this lack of dream material. From time to time she runs into Effi on the street with her child in a baby carriage, in a stroller, on a child's balance bike, and finally holding his hand, then the child with his own bicycle, the child with a school satchel, the child alone on his way home, lost in thought, dawdling – this strange, totally unfamiliar child. And Effi and Teresa pass each other with a nod in greeting, or they raise their hands, nothing more. And there are also days when they don't greet each other at all. There is the day after which they won't ever greet each other again. In the first years of her analysis Teresa talked about these encounters, then less often, and then not at all any more. But at one particular session, for whatever reason, she again remembered Effi's dream, and she talked about it. She retold the dream – Effi had dreamed that we were on the tram together; we were standing by the ticket machine, and I was next to her and suddenly I was very small, a tiny being, as small as a dwarf, and she bent down, picked me up and put me into her coat pocket – and as she was recounting it almost exactly in Effi's words, she remembered that Doctor Gupta knew Effi. That in all likelihood he also knew this dream. And of all the people about whom she tells him, session after session, Effi was the only one about whom he knew quite a bit, even though he may not have known everything, and he could picture her in person, in three dimensions and real. Effi's green eyes and her crooked smile; the expressive gestures of her hands – as if Effi were the one colourful figure in a series of black-and-white figures, as if she were a pulsatingly alive person in the midst of the dead.

Doctor Gupta is a reserved, almost passive man. He leaves almost all questions unanswered, leaves almost all of them open as if he felt that there was no one valid answer for any single question and no truly compelling reason for any decision. He evidently doesn't think that you can think anything through to its conclusion; perhaps he assumes that a new difficulty would come to light behind every insight arrived at. He leaves Teresa alone in her thicket of conjectures and haphazard assessments, and yet in spite of that it is important that he is there, on the periphery, a vague figure, but a figure of a certain size. During the session in which Teresa talked about Effi's dream, she suddenly thought she knew what it was that Effi was actually dreaming – Effi was dreaming about putting her, Teresa, into her pocket.

Turning her into a dwarf, making her tiny, causing her to disappear once and for all. That's what Effi had dreamed, and when Teresa arrived at that conclusion, Doctor Gupta, behind her, made a sound that was doubtless one of affirmation, of pleased agreement, almost a tender compliment.

That autumn the birds flock early; the wind tears the flocks apart, but they re-gather and become smaller, more distant, and then move off. The trouble spots of war move elsewhere and borders shift, the flood of refugees increases; far, far away typhoons destroy entire regions, and epidemics break out and die down. There is a book by Bunin on Doctor Gupta's desk. He has cut the delicate orange flowers growing in clay pots on the French balcony and put them into a vase on his desk, and covered the clay pots with branches. This painstaking care tells Teresa something about him. The number of insights is small: the revelation with regard to Effi's dream, insights about one thing or another; and Teresa thinks that at this rate she won't arrive at any clear idea or get to the bottom of anything essential. She might talk about it with Doctor Gupta; he would for a long time say nothing; then he might say that this was acceptable. That one could live with this after all.

The East

They arrived in Odessa at six in the morning. Ari says, I didn't sleep at all. I didn't sleep a wink, not one second. Seven lousy hours lying on my back submitting to this torture.

Jessica knows this isn't so. He did sleep; not long, it's true, but on and off. He slept while the train was taking them east through the night; she slept too. Their compartment had two beds across from each other with daytime coverlets of threadbare tapestry, little nightlights at the head ends above stacks of three firm pillows, and for each of them there was a linen runner to put on the small table. Jessica had put hers in her bag. Ari had spread his on the table; the runner was blue with delicate lighter woven stripes. They had peeled oranges on the runner. Ari had gone off and come back with a glass of tea in a silver holder, lumps of sugar the size of small chocolate bars. They had looked out at the unfamiliar landscape until it got dark. Ari was the first to get undressed and stretch out on his bed; he was the first to fall asleep. There's no point in telling him.

In Odessa it is still dark at six in the morning and there's a sickle moon in the sky above the train station roof. It's cold, but Jessica read somewhere that September at the Black Sea can be golden, that only the nights are cold; the days will surely still be warm. The other passengers get off the train and immediately walk away, hurrying along the station platform and disappearing at the end of the tracks to the right or left; there's no one being picked up and no one who would tarry or just stand there; everyone has a destination. Ari knows that there are old women at the train stations who rent out lodgings. It used to be that way before, why should it be any different nowadays; as long as there are still train stations and old women on earth, this won't change. The old women hold up cardboard signs with the words Lodgings or Room for the Night.

He says, We'll pick one.

And indeed, there inside the train station concourse are the old women with their cardboard signs. There are several – Jessica hadn't expected they would see even one. But there must have been at least twenty, and they were not at all alike. Which one are we going to take? At least they agree on which ones they don't want to pick. Not the 'madam' and not the alcoholic. Ari rejects any signs of religious symbols, certainly not the old one with the silver cross around her neck, and under no circumstances the one in the mangy fur coat. The old women stand silently in the station hall, some walk back and forth a little, just two or three steps in one direction then a couple of steps in another; they don't talk to each other, and they don't accost anyone. Their cardboard signs are creased, and the writing on them is faded and hard to read, it's possible they don't even say, Room for the Night, Lodgings; perhaps they say something completely different.

Indulgence.

Expectation. Or Annihilation.

Jessica has no idea why only words like that come to mind.

Not one of the old women is anything like what Ari had expected, had imagined – he'd say he hadn't imagined anything; it was simply too perilous to imagine anything beforehand. There aren't any who look like what Jessica is after. An old woman like those in the fairy tales: kind, serious. Extinct; they don't exist any more; at least they don't rent out rooms any more.

That one, we'll take that one there, Ari says.

A thin woman with short ash-grey hair, wearing a tracksuit and trainers, jacket closed; hands clasped.

We'll take her.

Ari bargains.

Jessica puts down her backpack and looks around the train station. There's a waiting room as large as a theatre, rows of chairs one behind the other, at the entrance a woman in uniform standing at a desk that's bare except for a telephone, and in front of the door leading out to the tracks, a heavy raspberry-red curtain. Enter: The Distant Land. Jessica had wanted to go to Odessa; Ari hadn't. Ari hadn't wanted to go to Odessa; in his opinion Odessa had nothing to offer except for the military and prostitution, pigeon droppings and a dirty sea. He came along in spite of that, out of kindness. To please Jessica. The old woman holds a crumpled pad in one hand and is writing numbers on it with a pencil stub; Ari takes the pencil stub from her and crosses out the numbers, writes down different numbers. She takes back the pencil stub and crosses out the numbers Ari has written. After a while they find a number they both like.

OK, let's go, Ari says. We'll go with her.

Night still hangs over the city; the streets are deserted. They walk three abreast, the old woman on the left, Jessica in the middle, Ari on the right. The old woman is in a hurry. She doesn't try to start a conversation with them; she doesn't say anything. Jessica can't possibly imagine – and, unlike Ari, she likes to imagine things, she's constantly imagining things – that this woman would have a room to rent in which she, Jessica, would like to spend any time. With a really clean bed, white, starched sheets and rustling down quilts, a table with chairs, and outside the window lovely scenery, not to mention a bouquet of anemones, a carafe of cold water, a bowl of berries. This old woman looks as if she doesn't even have a room of her own, has nothing of her own except the crumpled pad and pencil stub. She doesn't look as if she had a key in her trouser pocket, and there's something haphazard and hopeless about her tracksuit. But it's possible that she isn't – isn't evil; Jessica thinks she can judge this: the old woman isn't devious or contemptuous; she's just indifferent, resigned. Jessica hurries along the dark street next to her and Ari, and she says the one word she can say in this language; she says *Chernomorsky*. The old woman nods and points to the left, vaguely down the street somewhere; it seems she doesn't think this is important. Back there. Somewhere. There. As if the Black Sea were some minor little thing, something that could be anywhere.

The old woman says, *Uliza. Franzuski. Uliza Franzuski*. She says it once more; obviously they're supposed to remember it. She doesn't say it a third time. She stops in front of a metal door, the only door in an infinitely long wall. She points up and down the street; at the end of the street two figures are sweeping up the fallen plane tree leaves with birch brooms. Jessica can hear the swish of the brooms on the pavement. There's nothing else to be heard. The old woman resolutely pushes open the metal door, and they step inside. It is getting light now, and the inner courtyard behind the wall is bathed in an unreal brightness. Low wooden barracks, one next to another; a blonde prostitute is sitting in front of one of them, rolling a cigarette;

she's wearing a nightgown and green high-heeled shoes, and she looks as if she just got up. Grey cats roam around plastic bowls of leftovers; wild grape vines grow on the wire netting stretched over the courtyard, turning it into a big cage. On the right is a new building of unpainted concrete. The old woman guides them to the wooden barrack next to the blonde prostitute's barrack, and the blonde prostitute turns away, but says something first to Jessica. Something hard to understand. Hard to interpret.

The old woman opens the door and points wordlessly into the interior of the barrack. Dark, maybe there's a piece of furniture by the wall; it's hard to make out anything. A torn towel on the floor.

Jessica says, This won't do. Ari; I can't do this. Absolutely not. Totally impossible; I'm sorry.

Ari says, Because of the hooker or what.

Jessica says, Not just because of the hooker.

Ari says, I told you so. This is Odessa, I said so earlier.

The prostitute lights her crooked cigarette and yawns indulgently, smiles. She gets up, disappears into her little house, and comes back out with a canary-yellow sweater that she drapes over her naked shoulders. The old woman tries to divert Jessica's gaze from the prostitute back into the barrack.

Jessica says, No. She shakes her head; she raises her hands and says, No. I'm sorry.

Several times.

The old woman hesitates; then she turns around and goes over to the new building. She tugs on a rope next to the door, and a bell shrills inside the new building. The old woman crosses her arms on her chest, staring at something lying at her feet, and waits.

Ari says, Shit.

The door opens and a fat woman in velvet pyjamas comes out, complaining noisily and swinging a huge bunch of keys. She pushes the old woman aside, kicks at the cats, and cursing unlocks the other barracks, all of them, one after the other, every single one. Light on, light out. This one. Not this one? Then this one. This one, or if not, then this one. Well now, which one. She points to a large plastic box in a corner of the courtyard and looking at Jessica, says, Toilet. She shows numbers with her fingers, any old numbers. The prostitute is leaning against the wall of her little house and smoking with her eyes closed. The old woman is now sitting on a dirty plastic chair with her hands in her lap.

Come inside, Ari says. At least have a look at it.

Jessica is afraid that once she's inside the fat woman is going to slam the door shut and lock it from the outside. That she's going to lock them inside.

What for? Why ever.

Come inside, Ari says.

This barrack is a little larger than the others, and it actually has some light. There's a double bed in the corner with a dusty mattress on it and next to it a cupboard with bare glass shelves. On top of the cupboard sits a spooky teddy bear. Next to the bed, an American refrigerator. Ari opens the refrigerator; it is empty and black with mould. He closes the refrigerator and turns around to Jessica.

He says, Well then.

Jessica says, Well, I can't handle this. I'm too old for this. We're both too old for this; you must feel the same way; you can't want to stay here.

She points around at things. She points to the bear. She tries to imagine just how she's supposed to lie down in the evening with Ari in this bed. How she's supposed to read her book in this bed. The walls are thin. The prostitute will go about her business; she won't be the only blonde prostitute here. Jessica considers this room a punishment, but unlike Ari she doesn't think she should be punished. What for?

She says, Let's go. Let's get out of here somehow, all right? Let's try to get out of this place; let's just go, I beg you.

The old woman looks over at them from where she's sitting on her chair; she leans forward a tiny bit in the process. Not curious. Casually. The fat woman is whispering with the prostitute. She spits on two fingers and rubs at something on her pyjamas. They're all waiting. Ari braces himself against the refrigerator and pushes it away from the wall and towards the door.

He says, Could you help me, Jessica. Could you please switch on your brain?

Jessica has no inkling how she is supposed to help.

The fat woman comes running over to the barrack; she comes inside; she lifts up the electric cord of the refrigerator and shows it to them; she plugs it into an outlet above the baseboard; she says, *Functional*. OK? *Functional*.

Ari says, Yes, but that's not the problem. The refrigerator has got to go. It's got to go.

He pulls the plug out of the wall again and pushes the refrigerator farther towards the door; the refrigerator gets stuck in the doorway, and the fat woman pushes against it from outside. Jessica can see out into the courtyard through the window; she can see that the old woman has at least gotten up off her chair. The morning sun sets everything alight, and the dull hair of the prostitute – who has crossed one leg over the other and, cigarette in a corner of her mouth, is extensively scratching her ankles – almost gleams. Ari kicks the refrigerator through the door, right past the fat woman and into the courtyard. The fat woman shakes her head, refusing to believe this; the expression in her eyes as she looks at Ari is too incredulous to be hateful, but it wouldn't take much.

Ari opens the refrigerator door and points inside. Points inside for five seconds. Then he slams the door shut and gestures dismissively.

What are you waiting for, Ari yells. You wanted to get out of this place, so come on now, dammit, Jessica, get a move on.

Jessica reaches for her backpack. For a moment she doesn't know where she left it, but there it is, and she grabs it. She tries one more time to see it all differently – the prostitute, the barracks, the fat woman, the light, the wild grape vines ... to see the entire morning again differently; she knows that this is actually possible. You can almost always see everything in the world either one way or another. But she can't manage it here. She simply can't.

Together they go back out into the street, Jessica, Ari and the old woman, and behind them the metal door clangs heavily shut. Ari puts his hand into his trouser pocket, takes out some money and gives the old woman something, and she takes the money without counting it, as a matter of course and as if a successful, exacting presentation had taken place and was now concluded. She says neither thank you nor anything else; she goes back to the train station.

Jessica and Ari walk in the opposite direction, maybe the Black Sea lies in that direction. *Chernomorsky*. From time to time they turn around and watch the old woman walking in the middle of the street under the plane trees, free.

Jessica says, I wonder what she's thinking.

She's not thinking anything, Ari says. She's not thinking anything at all, Jessica. She's going back to the train station to wait for the next train. That's what she's doing. And that's all. Nothing more than that.

He says, We'll go down to the sea. We'll find something nice; I promise. I promise you.

The Return

Ricco has been gone for seven years, and now he's back and would like me to listen to him. This isn't necessarily easy for me. Oh, it's not as if I resented his leaving, not at all. It was right that he should have left. It's just that Ricco, once he starts to talk, can't stop – he talks without inter-ruption and as if there were no tomorrow. He talks about himself and all the inconceivable, incredible things that life has cooked up for him; he has to relate every single one, and in the process he forgets that I'm even there. That I exist on this earth too, that I too have a life, and that things happen to me too that I might like to talk about at some point.

I have known Ricco since we were children. We grew up in

the same housing development, went to the same schools; in the evening our mothers used to call us inside in the same tone of voice. But, in contrast to my father, Ricco's father had blown himself up while he was experimenting in his basement workshop, and Ricco had been there, and since then he's been wounded somehow. This is no secret. Ricco talks to everyone about it; he talks about it the way other people say that they like eating mussels, or that they go to the seaside every summer. He says, My father died when I was seven years old; he accidentally blew himself up, and I was there, and since then I can't stop thinking about it.

Ricco is now more than forty years old.

We both left the suburbs to go and live in the city, and in the city we never lost sight of each other. In the winter when Ricco couldn't pay his bills and they turned off his gas and electricity, he would come to me, and this happened frequently. When he was deeply and unhappily in love, he would also come to me, and that happened just as regularly. He turned dramatic when he was lovelorn; he cried uncommonly often for a man. He would tack a three-by-four-metre-large piece of packing paper up on his kitchen wall and in red crayon write on it the words that reminded him of the woman who had left him, all sorts of words. Street, beer, sleeping, midnight, Mercedes Benz, highway exit, lighter, stamps, stroll, ringing alarm clock, icy cold, no end in sight. He told me that once the paper got full, he would write on the wall, but before it ever got to that point, he had stopped and was devoting himself to another woman. It's possible that Ricco carried on this way because he knew a lot about sorrow – it was familiar territory for him, he kept wanting to be immersed again in the same kind of grief and the same sort of panic he had experienced as a child. Perhaps he assumed it might still change something.

When we were young and lived in the city, we drank a great deal. I drank a great deal, and Ricco drank twice as much. We were sliding downhill fast, things were going haywire; we lost track. At some point it got to be too much. Then I became pregnant; Ziggy was born, and Ricco left. He left from one day to the next; I think he left after – dead drunk and without a driver's licence – he had tried to park a car that wasn't his in front of a synagogue, and the police officers who were guarding the synagogue asked him to get out of the car and stood him up against the wall. He went up North and worked in a fish factory and on the big trawlers and finally on oil rigs. He made a lot of money, more than any of us had ever earned. He went into business for himself as a carpenter; with the money he made he bought himself a boat, a car, a house and a living room sofa set, and once he had his sofa set, he would sit down on it every evening and phone me.

He would say, It's me, Ricco. How are you?

Ricco has a talent for telling stories. He can be funny; he exaggerates in the right places; he jumps up and demonstrates things; he imitates voices and illustrates his story with gestures and with expletives. Up there in the North he would sit on his sofa with his feet up on his coffee table and say, Guess what I'm drinking, and I would say, No idea, and he would say, proudly, I'm drinking chocolate milk. During that period when he was working in the fish factory, on the trawlers and the oil rigs, he had stopped with the alcohol. I said, Terrific. And then he took a breath and told me about everything. He talked about the helicopter in which he had flown over the Bering Sea, and how in the helicopter he always sat way back by the turbine; he said, It's warm by the turbine, it's the best place if you're cold and you're bone tired. He said, pointlessly, Do you know what it's like when the water is so clear that you can see the whales? You can really see them, far, far down on the deep bottom of the sea. But it's even better if you actually close your eyes and don't look at all. The best thing is when it's enough for you to know what you could see if you wanted to. Do you understand what I mean?

He told about the oil rigs, about sleeping in a container, the carpenters' jokes about women and fucking, cunts and asses, always the same, until sleep overpowered them all, and all night long the roaring of the icy wind around the containers. Working twelve hours a day. With the money I bought a car, he said, a Chevrolet Suburban. Offroad. Silver. Not new. V8 Big Block. 6.5 Litre turbodiesel. He said the words one at a time and carefully, putting a period after each word, each phrase. He did an impressive imitation of the crazy engine of his new car, and then he described the view he had from his picture window of the Skerries and the Sound, of the colourful boats and the night-time sea.

He said, I'll let you know when the beam of light from the lighthouse comes in here. Wait. It's coming – now. And – now. And – now.

He said, Shall I tell you something? I'm a happy man.

And then one day he phoned and said, I'm lonely. The people here think I'm a freak. The people here work for their wives and children, for their one-family houses, family cars, family vacation trips, and they ask me, What about you? What are you working for. No idea what I should tell them. I have no idea. Do you realise that we've known each other, you and I, since we were children? We knew each other before we were grown up, and something about that seems so very important to me; I just can't quite put my finger on what it is. It snows here all the time. I constantly have the feeling that tomorrow is Christmas. Come to visit me. No one ever comes to visit me; how can that possibly be true. I'm living here in the best place on earth, and no one comes to see me. Why is this. Can you tell me why it should be this way? Why don't you come to see me?

And I started and tried to say that I had my own life here to cope with, a life without whales and without the Sound, but Ricco wasn't even listening. That was the problem – he couldn't listen. Sometimes, while he was talking, I would put the receiver down on the table and go wash the dishes, and when I came back and held the receiver up to my ear again, he was still talking about his fishing rods and his neighbours and the Maglite he had just bought, and he hadn't even noticed that I had been gone. And on the whole, this doesn't matter. It doesn't matter at all. I know what Ricco wants to tell me anyway, and I understand the way he thinks. There's a strange connection between his head and my head; it's always been that way. I remember everything he says, and I also remember what he says while I'm washing the dishes. He told me about the girl he picked up that Saturday evening in the city; he told me how drunk she was, too drunk to take off her shoes by herself, too drunk to go to bed with him. And so Ricco simply sat on the edge of her bed and looked at her all night long until it got light outside. When it was light and she opened her eyes, he was still sitting there like that, and she said, Will you stay a little while longer, and he said, Of course. Why not?

If he were to ask me, Do you still remember how often she dropped the key outside her apartment? I'd say, Three times.

And if he'd say, Do you still remember which blouse she was wearing, then I can tell him that it was a white blouse with puffed sleeves gathered with embroidery, and that this reminded him of something that happened long ago.

Ricco says, I don't want to fuck at all. I just want to be touched.

I say, I know.

And now he's here again. He has sold his company, his car, his house and all his fishing rods and has come back. It was too lonely up there. He bought a new house in the same area where we grew up, a house not far away from the housing development in which we were children, not

far from the place where his father is buried. Ricco is here
again; he has come to visit me and sits the entire evening on
my sofa staring at Ziggy who has gotten quite big, a regular,
genuine, big boy. Ricco taps the sofa next to him and says to
Ziggy, Come here; and Ziggy isn't a child who needs to be
begged; he just goes right over to him.

Ricco says, Do you know that I've known you from the
time you were a baby? That I've known your mama since
she was a baby? A fat, round, friendly baby?

Ziggy politely acts as if he could imagine it, and Ricco and
I both have to laugh. The three of us have supper together,
and Ricco comes to sit with us when I read to Ziggy. Ziggy
is eight years old; he still wants me to read to him, and I'm
hoping he will want me to do that for a good while longer.

The sentences in Ziggy's books used to be simple. The
lion met a rabbit. Once upon a time there was a king. One
day the bear got sick and stayed in his cave. Nothing easier
than that, said the grasshopper. Nothing easier than that!
Today the sentences are already grown up and complex. A
cold wind blew from the northeast; their course led north-
ward; the water was ice cold; they walked on in their wet
clothes.

Ricco listens and all the time he is looking around at
Ziggy's room. He looks at Ziggy's globe, the Titanic he built
by himself out of cardboard, his little guitar. He looks at
Ziggy's years.

I drink a glass of wine; Ricco drinks hot water. He wants
to tell me everything – about his departure, about the day

when he pulled the door of his house on the Sound shut behind him for the last time, about his new house, his plans for the future. He wants to tell me again about his father. He looks quite different from the way he did back then; he has become strong, and he's brought back a sizeable belly from the North; back then he was slender and boyish, energetically charged somehow. I don't want to know in what way I look different.

Getting up from the kitchen table, I say, Can you tell me about it tomorrow? I'd like to go to sleep now. I have to work tomorrow, and Ziggy has to go to school early.

Ricco looks surprised. He looks at me; then he looks away. He says, Where will I sleep; and I say, You'll sleep in my bed, and I'll sleep in Ziggy's bed.

Ricco lies down in my bed; he leaves the light on, and the door wide open. I wash the dishes and sweep the kitchen; I lie down next to the sleeping Ziggy, and then I have to get up again to change the water in Ziggy's goldfish tank; the fish keep coming up to the surface of the water, and I can't stand the sound they make gasping for air. Ricco sees me walk through the hall with the goldfish bowl, and he sits up in my bed and says, What are you doing there. What on earth are you doing?

I stop and stand there; I think that in all its simplicity this is hard to explain. I'd like to say, Do you still remember when we were children and we went into the forest and held long birch sticks to the power line? How it hummed inside us then, a humming in our entire bodies, from our toes all the way up to our scalps, and to this day I haven't gotten rid of the humming; that's what I'd like to say, but although I know what Ricco is thinking, Ricco doesn't always know what I'm thinking. The light is already out in the hall, and the two fish in the glass bowl between my hands shimmer like gold leaf.

Intersections

She told Vito at breakfast. She didn't have to say anything; she could have kept it to herself; it's unlikely that Vito and André would ever run into each other. That André might then say, Listen, Vito, Patricia phoned me to complain about my tenants, and I told her that if she didn't like my tenants, she should buy the house. I said to Patricia, Buy the house. Didn't she tell you? It's unlikely that there would ever be such an encounter. So she needn't have told Vito about the conversation with André, she needn't have mentioned it. Why, in spite of that, did she mention it. Why did she say, I spoke on the phone with André. I called him up to tell him about the situation here, and instead he told me about his own situation; for half an hour he complained about his miserable, dreary suffering. And right at the end, when he was almost finished and I was practically slipping off my chair with boredom and weariness, he said he'd be willing to sell us the house. I'm sorry, he said, but I'd have to ask a good bit for it. That's what he said.

She told Vito at breakfast at eight in the morning on a Saturday; they were sitting across from each other at the kitchen table; Patricia had rubbed and scrubbed the table-top until the wood surface turned silvery and velvety – wood like a dull mirror. Vito had got up early to go out and buy the paper; he had boiled two eggs, put the tea on the teapot warmer, and turned on the radio, then said three seconds later, I think I'd better turn it off again, Pat; let me turn off the goddamn fucking radio; he turned the radio off again. Then he was slicing the bread. He listened to Patricia with an amiable, calm expression quite rare for him.

Patricia said, André is sick; he won't last much longer.

She was thinking, Each and every sentence I think is an abyss. Should I say it this way, or in a different way, or would it be best not to say it at all. Blue-grey? Or grey-blue. I shouldn't be merely weighing every word, I should be weighing every single syllable, the individual letters, the breath I have to take in order to speak, the sleep I need so that I can think. How dangerous this life can suddenly become again.

She said, So, here's the story, André won't last much longer. He needs money for medicine. He is going to die.

For that reason nothing matters a damn to him any more. He is dying.

André had moved out of the house next door a year ago. Had moved to a place near a hospital with cardiologists, ultrasound machines, osteopaths. In your middle years you move to a house at the edge of the forest; when you're old there are different priorities. A tall, fat man with a broken nose and arms that are too long. Patricia can still see him walking down the meadow to the forest to check on his fence, a melancholy ape in red overalls, and calling back over his shoulder, he says, Tell your guy not to keep taking the branches out of the fence to throw into your stove; the fence is alive; the branches are part of the fence; and she can see Vito giving André the middle finger behind his back. No close ties. They never went over there; they never invited André to their house. Conversations were only held over the fence or in the autumn while raking leaves on the street, or at the borderline of the property, always careful to keep their distance. Towards the end he suddenly had a Chinese wife, fetched or sent for from a catalogue or from the airport, a Chinese wife with a hairless dog who had to be smeared with suntan lotion in the midday heat, a sight that, as Vito said several times, made him want to puke. Then they moved away, and André rented out the house and the antisocials moved in.

Did you know that their son broke into our place, Patricia had said to André on the telephone, had said to André wherever he was, on the outskirts of some city; the connection was poor with a gurgling on the line as if André were dipping the receiver into a pail of water every now and then, only to shake it vigorously for a while before continuing to shout into it. Steven Gonzales Soderberg. He broke into our house. That's an untenable situation; can you imagine it?

They had been away for a week and when they came back home, around midnight, Vito stepped on broken glass in the entrance hall before he'd even turned on the light. The side window had first been smashed and then forced open, and the door to the hallway was wide open, and all the things in the house had been turned upside down, their things had been turned inside out. Torn cushions and pillows, a flurry of bed feathers. Pictures pulled off the walls and torn from their frames – as if people were still hiding money behind etchings these days. There were also installations, photographs of Patricia, of Pat when she was young, with that reserved face she still has occasionally even now; only nowadays her reserve points in a totally different direction, no longer to a possible revelation; in any case, photographs of Pat in her young years spread out on the floor of her workroom, and the table in front of the concealed door, behind which there was actually nothing except the dusty attic, had not been simply turned or kicked over, but carefully moved to one side. And yet, alcohol and sugar syrup had been poured out, shelves turned over, and chairs kicked to pieces, the whole shooting match, except no faeces on the kitchen table, and you could sense that one person had been in the house alone, someone with enough time who possibly had sat down for quite a while in Patricia and Vito's kitchen and imagined how it would feel to be someone else.

The antisocials had moved in with suitcases, not with a moving van, just with suitcases; André had rented them the house furnished; presumably they didn't have any furniture, no possessions, no belongings. A woman with four children, three girls and a teenage boy, and there was also a father who had been picked up by the police that first week after some incredible yelling and screaming; and apparently it wasn't the woman who'd called the police, but one of the girls, the oldest, a thin, hunched-over figure in pyjamas standing on the street in the early dawn shouting curses after the police van as it drove off with her father until it turned the corner.

The antisocials trashed the garden in no time; they threw the furniture out of the windows and got themselves three cats and a big dog; they would start up the circular saw without sawing anything, and the saw would screech pointlessly into the quiet afternoon. Patricia had no problems with their garbage and the yelling and the saw. She had problems with the expression on the woman's face as she stood in front of the house waiting for the dog to finish his business, that satisfied and self-absorbed expression on the woman's bloated face dreamy from medications.

On some days, after the children had got on the school bus, the father would come back holding himself stiffly erect, and of course they didn't close the windows; you could hear everything. Animals. Sometimes the teenager, Steven Gonzales, would stand at night under the street lamp with his back to the house, smoking. Or he would ride figure eights on his bicycle in front of the garden gate for hours and hours. Didn't say hello. Didn't even raise a hand in greeting, but Patricia knew that he was looking at her, and she knew that he'd once been an intelligent child.

Did you know that their son broke into our house, Patricia had asked André on the phone, and surprisingly André had said, Yes, yes, I knew; I was told about it. And for a moment Patricia didn't know what to say – I was told about it. Who told you about it, and if you knew, how could you ignore it?

She said, These people have to go. I'm telling you in Vito's words; it's what Vito thinks; these people have got to go. Those aren't my words, but it's what I think. It's what I want. It's only a question of time, you understand? The next time he'll come over when we're at home; I don't dare go down to the lake by myself any more. I don't dare go out into the garden alone after dark. That's no way to live. Do you follow me?

For the first time in her life she had called the police. She had called the police, and the police came at two o'clock at night, a huge policewoman and a sleepy, puny police-man, and they had collected fingerprints and written down everything and photographed it all. Later that same night, at three o'clock, the doorbell rang and it was the woman from next door, and with a triumphant voice she said, It was my son; my son did it, Steven Gonzales Soderberg, and I can't cope with him any more. She had pronounced her son's name as solemnly as if it were a precious object, as if it were all about a rare and marvellous exemplar of an extinct species. The police officer had placed the form for lodging a complaint on the kitchen table, and Patricia had said, May I sleep on this for a night and think it over; I have to think about it; the officer had looked at her as if she were a hopeless case.

What is there to think about. About Steven Gonzales?

Yes, about Steven Gonzales. About Steven Gonzales Soderberg, dammit, Patricia had said. I have to think about him; I've never brought a charge against anyone before; I don't want to be responsible for his getting fucked in the ass in jail, if you know what I mean; she'd begun to feel extremely hot; she had looked past the police officer, watching Vito as he led the woman to the door, pushed the woman towards the door, making sure to keep his distance. The woman had left an organic smell in their kitchen that she hadn't been able to get rid of since. In the end Patricia did press charges. Of course she had pressed charges; she had written it out and had signed a statement saying that she wanted to see Steven Gonzales Soderberg appear before a judge; she had put every single one of the letters of his name on the scale. Sixteen years old. With ears that stuck out, badly cut hair, bags under his eyes, a shifty look. Wiry. No prospects, nowhere.

André's voice on the telephone. Complaining, monotonous. He would never be able to get those people out. No one more unhappy about the situation than he was. He had rented the house furnished; not a single piece of furniture was intact; all the garden tools, gone; sold no doubt: the electric pruning shears, the lawnmower, the drills. The knife collection, a suitcase full of Chinese knives, and who has them now? Well? Who would have them? Patricia could have three guesses.

He said, I'll give you three guesses. There's nothing to be done, nothing at all. I can't get them out; if they're ever to go away, you have to buy the house; with a change in house ownership they can be thrown out. It's just that I'd have to ask quite a bit for it. The roof and the heating system. You know. Will he come before a judge? Won't he be put away in any event?

No, he won't come before a judge, Patricia had said. Of course not. The break-in will go on his record; he is sixteen years old; in such a case there's nothing you can do. If he bashes in my head in revenge for my having brought charges against him – then he would come before a judge. Then he'd come before a judge, and André at the other end of the line, had laughed at that, a booming and at the same time an affected laugh.

Patricia watches Vito as he puts the teapot back on the teapot warmer, the handle of the pot carefully turned towards her. She just sits there, she's not hungry, she isn't tired and isn't fully awake, for a moment she is in an in-between state, something light, resounding, as if hovering on the verge of a realisation.

Vito says calmly, There is no alternative, Patricia. We will buy the house, and we have to do it quickly before that idiot André comes to his senses and asks for more money. There's nothing to think over; it's a stroke of luck. Just think of the garden, take a look at it from upstairs. The house is big. The barn is huge.

But I'd like to think it over, Patricia says. I have to put my mind to it; I'd like to be able to justify it morally, ethically. They've got to go somewhere, these people have to have a place to live; I don't want them as neighbours, but neither do I want them to fetch up on the street.

But morality doesn't come into this, Vito says. You can forget your idiotic moral standards, besides people like these will always find a place to live. Once they're gone, you're going to have to fumigate the house, to fumigate it from cellar to attic; you can start worrying about that. Nothing else. Call André. Tell him we'll buy the house. We'll buy his house today.

Patricia says nothing. She looks across the table past Vito through the room; the linoleum floor gleams like a body of water; the sun is now up above the trees; the sun's rays fall at a slant through the bay window, onto the table, onto the flowers in the vase on the table; God shows himself at Vito's back, silent and emphatic in the deep blue of the hyacinths.

Mother

Half asleep, my mother had written in her diary, I'm lying on my back half asleep, watching my life pass before my eyes. A succession of days that will pass ever more quickly from year to year. When I'm lying on my back at three o'clock at night half asleep and see my life pass before me, I lose all eagerness for, and confidence in, the future. And tomorrow? The world will look different.

She was twenty when she wrote this in her diary, neatly and carefully in her – back then and even into old age – girlish handwriting. I was fifteen when I read this diary, by accident and surreptitiously, and then when I turned the page, there was only one single sentence on the next page, written diagonally across the paper with a red pen;

this sentence, in large and seemingly outraged letters: I am afraid.

I closed the book, almost dropped it as if I had burned myself.

My mother grew up in the city on a quiet street lined by plane trees; a long row of identical blocks of flats; she grew up with her mother and two older brothers in a three-room flat; she played in the rear courtyards that ran endlessly into one another, in the laundry rooms, and in the attics. Her best girlfriend was named Margo Rubinstein, and my mother and Margo Rubinstein together kept a yellow notebook in which they wrote down aspects of their physical characteristics, of the persons they were, and the persons they would be or could be.

You are – Margo noted the key points – small and dainty, thin lips and freckles beneath your face powder, hair short like Audrey's in *Roman Holiday*, perhaps glossy black. Somewhat quiet, but intelligent. Predilection for foreign words; you read the newspaper! Love angora wool sweaters, bergamot perfume and Bakelite necklaces. Slow lazy movements, your expression: attractively sleepy, a slight squint, ears sticking out a little?

My mother was an athletic girl with long brown hair that she wore in a braid fastened on top of her head. Her expression was alert, shy, amiable and stubborn. She wrote, You are as tall as my brothers, curly hair down to your chin and platinum blonde, grass-green eyes, lashes like a porcelain doll, and you absolutely have to smoke, Senoussi Orient cigarettes, with an amber cigarette holder. Negligee, velvet slippers with pompoms, and toe nails with coral nail polish. Laughter like a glockenspiel! Cheeky, a heartbreaker.

They wrote these sentences into their yellow notebook in Margo's mother's room. Margo's mother's room was cool and crepuscular; the window always open a crack, and the curtain moving in the wind, changing the light. Along one wall stood a wide bed with a shiny quilt on it; across from the bed, a make-up table with an oval mirror; furs and tulle skirts were crammed inside the clothes closet; a slight aroma of sandalwood, pepper and vetiver hung in the air. It was strictly forbidden to enter this room. Margo and my mother wrote their sentences secretly and hurriedly into the notebook lying on their stomachs on a carpet on which lions were pursuing gazelles. Before they tiptoed out of the room again, they straightened the carpet fringes, placing a ruler against the fringes; they pushed the curtain one millimetre to the right and back again.

They wrote, You will be happy. You will have a great deal of money. You will go far away to America or to Australia; you will lead a rich life.

When she was sixteen, my mother graduated from school and began working for the city administration. She married my father when she was twenty, against her family's wishes, and moved with him into an apartment that was two houses away from the apartment in which she had grown up. She had five children, all of them girls.

Margo Rubinstein became a nurse. She started an affair
with a doctor and moved out of her mother's apartment
into a nurses' residence; the affair with the doctor lasted
three years; then it was over, and Margo moved back in
with her mother. She came to see us once or twice a month,
a raw-boned spinster in a fur coat that smelled of dust and
mothballs; and she allowed my father to take this coat from
her shoulders in a way that embarrassed me. Under the
coat she wore corduroy dresses and pearl necklaces, small
brooches in the shape of cat heads with red, feverish cat eyes
made of garnets. She drank tea with my mother, and she
always had a perplexed, apologetic expression on her face,
an expression halfway between embarrassment and irony,
as if she wanted to say she knew very well that everything
had gone wrong, even though it didn't have to go wrong
at all. That she herself knew and regretted it. Her eyes
were as round as circles, a deep brown, and outlined with
black eyeliner pencil. Her right front tooth seemed to be
getting longer and longer with the years; it clacked against
the teacup when she drank, and I had to avert my eyes.
My mother had told us that Margo Rubinstein had always
been the first to be asked to dance. The very first one, and
for her entire youth she had been pursued by a swarm of
boys; she had, my mother said, a unique way of turning her
head back over her shoulder to see who was following her,
and then looking away again and venturing a little smile, a
mysterious, lackadaisical, wonderful smile.

Margo Rubinstein spoke so slowly it seemed as if she
were under the influence of sleeping pills, and her hands

were pale and narrow, and cold. My mother's posture as she sat at the table with her indicated that she would not tolerate any silliness or impudence from us; when she'd had too much of our staring and giggling, she would get up and push us out the door.

On Margo's birthday my mother went to visit her. She came back around ten o'clock and told us, in answer to our questions, that she'd had supper with Margo and her mother and after that they had watched the news on television together. A birthday party that left us speechless, which we wanted to hear about over and over again – how could that be. Margo Rubinstein resembled some of the characters in books we'd read: sad old girls who lived with their mothers and hoped for deliverance.

What is her mother like? Mrs Rubinstein, what is she like? We asked our mother that, and she answered, Margo's mother is mean, but she's still Margo's mother.

Margo Rubinstein died when she was fifty years old, unmarried and childless; she died of cancer. She had continued to live with her mother, taking care of her, until the end. When Margo died, my mother took over that task. I don't know what Margo's death meant for my mother. I have no recollection of her grieving, and I don't think I ever spoke with her about it. Margo Rubinstein disappeared from our lives, and my mother now took care of Mrs Rubinstein in her stead. She did this for many years, and she always addressed Margo's mother the way she had in her childhood. She never addressed her by her first name, and she continued to address her formally as '*Sie*'. In our family the name Mrs Rubinstein took on the nature of a synonym.

My mother went to Mrs Rubinstein three times a week in the early evening after her work at the municipal office; once I picked her up from there. Mrs Rubinstein was sitting in an armchair in her living room in front of the television set. Her hair was carefully combed, tinted violet. She wore an ironed blouse and had a wool blanket over her knees on which her hands slid back and forth, feeling for something invisible. She was absorbed in a shopping programme, and I was able to look at her bedroom undisturbed: the mirror in whose oval my mother and Margo had looked at themselves forty years ago; I could tug on the fringes of the carpet on which the lions were killing the gazelles. Margo's room had also remained unchanged after her death. A girl's room. A narrow foldaway bed, a bookshelf and a porcelain cardinal bird on the night table.

My mother was washing the kitchen floor on her hands and knees. The doorbell rang, a charity organisation bringing Mrs Rubinstein her supper: bread and cold cuts and cheese. Make her some peppermint tea, my mother called from the bathroom. And I did and set everything down in front of Mrs Rubinstein. I asked her if she'd like to eat by herself or whether I should keep her company, and she said in a tone of voice I remember to the present day, that it was all the same to her. So I sat down near her because it was all the same to her whether she ate by herself or in company, and I watched as she devoured the bread, cold cuts and cheese, apathetically and without appetite, without any feeling. She drank the peppermint tea and never took her eyes off the TV screen, and then she began to cry, and when I talked with my mother about it later, my mother said, She's crying about Margo, she's crying about her only child.

My mother pushed the vacuum cleaner through Margo's room; she smoothed the bedspread on the folding bed and straightened the cardinal bird, and then she hung the washed dishtowels up outside on the balcony and watered the geraniums. She washed the cup from the peppermint tea and put the dishes for the charity out in the hall. While she was doing all this, she talked with Mrs Rubinstein; she talked about this and that, matter-of-factly but with solicitude in her voice, with warmth. She said, Don't stay up too late, Mrs Rubinstein. And don't cry so much. Go to bed early. Sleep eases everything. Until tomorrow then. I'll come again tomorrow.

Towards the end Mrs Rubinstein couldn't live alone any more. She was almost blind and could hardly hear anything; she fell and couldn't get up by herself, and she couldn't open the door for the charity people. A nephew three times removed turned up from somewhere and took things in hand and put Mrs Rubinstein into a home. He cleaned out the apartment in no time at all, and shortly before he turned over the key he permitted my mother to come by one last time to choose some small thing from among the stuff he had not yet sold. We accompanied our mother. We stood in the cellar around a cardboard box in which there were the ice skates with which, in the winter on the frozen lake, Margo Rubinstein as a young girl had turned graceful pirouettes, looking back over her shoulder in that inimitable way of hers. It was difficult to bear. I can't remember whether we took anything, whether my mother took anything. I assume she was looking for the yellow notebook; she didn't find it.

After the flat had been cleared out, during Mrs Rubinstein's first weeks in the home, my mother and father went on a long trip. They were gone four weeks; then, when they came back, my mother had to go to work; she had to do this and that; perhaps two months passed before she found the time to visit Mrs Rubinstein in the home together with my father. It was unusual for my mother to take my father along on such a visit; perhaps she was a little afraid, didn't think she could do it by herself. The home had a generous, bright common room, where seniors sat at round tables, whispering as they played solitaire; there was a friendly reception desk, an impressive aquarium and a conservatory full of bamboos and agaves. My mother and father went from the common room into the conservatory, to the reception desk and back; Mrs Rubinstein was nowhere to be seen. The room she had been assigned was empty. During their search for Mrs Rubinstein, my mother and father kept passing a figure sitting in a wheelchair near the foyer, a being in a wheelchair, and the fifth time they passed by, my father grabbed my mother's arm and said softly, That's her. That's Mrs Rubinstein.

No, my mother said emphatically; that's not her. Absolutely not.

The being in the wheelchair was a shrivelled, withered leaf. A living corpse, tiny and faded, almost defunct, with uncombed smoke-coloured hair projecting from her skull like bristly, tangled fur. But my mother took heart and spoke to her. She took one of the spectrally thin hands into her large, warm hand and spoke to her, and then she turned around to my father and said, Oh, you're right; it really is Mrs Rubinstein.

Mrs Rubinstein died shortly after that; she was buried next to her daughter, and my mother returned home from the funeral almost cheerful. And then, many years later she informed us that she had received news of the death of the nephew three times removed; the daughter of the nephew had sent her a death announcement, saying that he had died after a short, serious illness. At first this information perplexed my sisters and me; then it made us angry. What did Mrs Rubinstein's nephew three times removed and his daughter have to do with our mother; so we asked her, Can you tell us what these people have to do with you and why they sent you their death announcement? Why are they bothering you with that; why should you know about it.

But my mother ignored these questions. She quite clearly didn't consider these questions worth answering. She changed the subject and started talking about something else; she seemed to know, I later thought, that questions like that would sooner or later answer themselves.

She knew.